The Critics are Raving About
DOMENIC STANSBERRY!

"Suspense… illicit passion… murder… Stansberry does it with originality, through the freshness of his imagery and the lyricism of his lament."
— *The New York Times*

"Written in the tradition of Graham Greene… disquietingly black and totally absorbing."
— *Los Angeles Times*

"An enviable achievement."
— *San Francisco Chronicle*

"The real thing… Superb… Stansberry has done it again with this gut-wrenching tale… and he tells his story in the hard-edged prose it demands. Straight noir, no chaser."
— *Booklist*

"There's a lot in this bluntly articulate tale to like."
— *Publishers Weekly*

"A story of obsession and jealousy… hot and heavy… you won't be able to avert your eyes."
— *Mystery Book Line*

"Intriguing… Stansberry blends his ingredients with definite panache."
— *Publishers Weekly*

"Through a poetics of menace that at times takes on a positively hallucinatory beauty, Stansberry exposes the Manichaean heart of noir."
— *LA Weekly*

Sara and I had not undressed yet. She was in her office clothes, a skirt cut at the knees, a blouse that unbuttoned in the back. She ran her fingers on my collar, then down the length of my tie, touching my belt. Soon things between us grew feverish. I lifted her skirt. She clutched me tighter, excited. My tie was undone, and the end of it got tangled between us. I pulled the tie off and it snaked across her chest, and somehow it got wrapped around her wrist and my wrist, too.

"We've been meeting like this for a while now," she said.

"Not so long. A few weeks."

"It wasn't what I had planned, you know. This kind of thing, with a married man. I have a boyfriend."

"I know."

"He wants to get serious with me."

"You told me that, yes."

"So what are we going to do?"

She was astride me now, and I reached up to touch her breasts. My tie hung over her neck, draped like a scarf.

"Your wife, Elizabeth, she knows, doesn't she?"

"I don't think so."

"She will. Sooner or later."

I said nothing.

"So, what are you going to do? About us?"

Maybe that was the trigger. Sara's question.

I remember lying on my back, with Sara straddled over me. My grip was easy one instant, my hands gentle on her shoulders, then my grip tightened...

**OTHER BOOKS
BY DOMENIC STANSBERRY:**
CHASING THE DRAGON
THE LAST DAYS OF IL DUCE
MANIFESTO FOR THE DEAD
THE SPOILER
EXIT PARADISE

**OTHER HARD CASE CRIME BOOKS
YOU WILL ENJOY:**
GRIFTER'S GAME *by Lawrence Block*
FADE TO BLONDE *by Max Phillips*
TOP OF THE HEAP *by Erle Stanley Gardner*
LITTLE GIRL LOST *by Richard Aleas*
TWO FOR THE MONEY *by Max Allan Collins*
HOME IS THE SAILOR *by Day Keene* °
KISS HER GOODBYE *by Allan Guthrie* °

° coming soon

The
CONFESSION

by Domenic Stansberry

A HARD CASE CRIME NOVEL

A HARD CASE CRIME BOOK
(HCC-006)
November 2004

Published by

Dorchester Publishing Co., Inc.
200 Madison Avenue
New York, NY 10016

in collaboration with Winterfall LLC

*If you purchased this book without a cover, you should know
that it is stolen property. It was reported as "unsold and
destroyed" to the publisher, and neither the author nor the
publisher has received any payment for this "stripped book."*

Copyright © 2004 by Domenic Stansberry

Cover painting copyright © 2004 by R. B. Farrell

All rights reserved. No part of this book may be reproduced or
transmitted in any form or by any electronic or mechanical
means, including photocopying, recording or by any information storage and retrieval system, without the written
permission of the publisher, except where permitted by law.

*This book is a work of fiction. Names, characters, places, and
incidents either are the products of the author's imagination or
are used fictitiously, and any resemblance to actual events or
persons, living or dead, is entirely coincidental.*

ISBN 0-8439-5354-3

The name "Hard Case Crime" and the Hard Case Crime logo
are trademarks of Winterfall LLC. Hard Case Crime Books are
selected and edited by Charles Ardai.

Printed in the United States of America

Visit us on the web at www.HardCaseCrime.com

THE CONFESSION

Preface

Sometimes, I close my eyes and imagine myself at the top of Mt. Tamalpais, the jagged peak that overlooks Marin. The weather is temperate one moment, unruly and fog-driven the next. The wind blows through me as if I don't exist. There are rumors about this mountain. Of spiritualists who transcend the material world while walking the high trails. Of cougars sleeping in the grass. Of coyotes who grab small children and disappear into the rocks.

The gray Pacific lies to the west and San Francisco Bay to the east, and the land in between is multitudinous. Hardscrabble beaches. Green pastures and black forests. Brown hills and canyons filled with yellow light. The roads spiderweb down the hills, over the old Indian graveyards, past the abandoned communes and the Zen retreats. They snake beneath the custom homes that gleam on the promontories, through the old towns, past squares lined with madrone and eucalyptus and oak. All-American towns really, each one bleeding into the next.

It is a place where people find their inner selves, this mountain. Where they separate from the world.

Myself, I float over it all. Over the redwoods and the scrub oak. Over the roads that follow the old creeks, flowing through the subdivisions into the mudflats. I see the cars siphoning into 101, that gray ribbon that winds along the bay.

I see it all, I tell myself. I see everything.

My old house, my old life.

Elizabeth—alone by the water.

All visions are illusions, someone told me. At a cocktail

party, I think. A colleague of mine. All dreams are born in the darkness, he said, and there are times, even now, I feel that darkness within myself.

I open my eyes.

I am no longer on the mountain. I am far away. Another place, another time. My wife lies in the bed next to me.

Life is a circle, they say. We begin where we end. I no longer argue with such truisms. I close my eyes and find myself back where I started, on that dock there, on the far side of the mountain, clutching her necklace in my hand.

PART ONE

Sara and Elizabeth

I.

Some of you will remember this story. It was ten years ago, and I was employed then as a forensic psychologist in Marin County. Much of my work involved talking to criminals, then testifying as to their sanity in a court of law. On the afternoon this all began, for example—that afternoon when I blacked out in Sara Johnson's apartment—I was scheduled to examine a man who'd been accused of strangling his wife.

Because of that incident, and all that has happened since, I know many people will be suspicious of anything I put down here. Jake Danser is not to be trusted, they will say. I have ulterior motives. I pretend to be whole-hearted, confessing minor flaws to hide a deeper evil.

I am not innocent of everything, I admit. I was thirty-seven years old then, vain in the way of men at that stage of life, wanting to own the world and feeling that I'd reached a pivot point, a time of reckoning. At the same time, I had my own predilections and my own past, and these things bound me in ways hard to escape. Maybe those old emotions, coming again to the surface, triggered the incident that day at Sara's apartment. Or maybe the cause lay elsewhere. I don't know. I can't say for sure.

On that afternoon, I met with Sara Johnson at her apartment in Sausalito. Sara was an attorney, ten years younger than myself. She worked for the public defender's office, and we knew each other on account of a case I had taken regarding an aging schizophrenic who refused to take his medication. My testimony had kept him out of the asylum, and Sara admired me for this. She was a wholesome girl, idealistic and straightforward—except for the fact she'd been meeting with me these past weeks, surreptitiously, in back offices, elevators, closets. Furtive encounters that had been building in intensity, so now we were together in her apartment, having stolen away for the afternoon.

I made a couple of drinks, preparing them carefully. Vodka for her, gin for me.

She sighed deeply and went into the kitchen. When she came back, her glass was empty.

"That was quick."

"The Mori case, it's all anyone's talking about," she said. "Did you see that spread in the paper?"

"I did."

"Angela Mori was a beautiful woman," Sara said, and there was something like envy in her voice. She and the dead woman were about the same age, from similar backgrounds, with high cheekbones and the look of privilege. "You knew her, didn't you?"

"Let's not talk about Angela." I lowered my voice. There was a catch in it, the briefest stutter. "You're a beautiful woman yourself, you know."

"I'm alive, anyway. I have that going for me."

She turned to look outside, down the hill through the jumble of telephone wires that looped over the gray streets toward the harbor. If you looked hard, you could see the sailboats small and white on the bay. It was a typical Marin County day, a little windy and blue with the sun shining hard off the water and cars glinting by on the road below.

"Jake," she said. "What are we going to do?"

I circled behind her then and put my hand around her waist and placed my palm on her stomach, touching her white blouse. I kissed Sara's neck and felt her back arch toward me, and had for a moment the sensation of something shifting within my head, the blood rushing. I caught a glimpse of us in the mirror. Sara's blonde hair, her small breasts and long legs. My own blue eyes, my black hair: longish, just graying, pulled back in a pony. I put my hand down into her skirt, her eyes closed—and in that moment I thought about my wife.

"What are we going to do?" Sara asked again.

Though she was not a naive woman, it was a naive question. Her eyes were still closed. The look on her face said she was moving towards some secret place within. We fell onto the bed. There was a delicious coolness about her body, a tautness. My thoughts drifted. My wife again. Our beautiful house out at the point . . . our beautiful things. . . .

Then I thought about Angela Mori, and the morgue photos I'd seen splayed across the desk of her husband's attorney.

Sara and I had not undressed yet. She was in her office clothes, a skirt cut at the knees, a blouse that unbuttoned in the back. She ran her fingers on my collar, then down the length of my tie, touching my belt. Soon things between us grew feverish. I lifted her skirt. She clutched me tighter, excited. My tie was undone, and the end of it got tangled between us. I pulled the tie off and it snaked across her chest, and somehow it got wrapped around her wrist and my wrist, too.

"Your eyes," she said to me, "they have a life of their own. The way they glimmer."

"The window to the soul," I joked.

"Do you believe in it?"

"What?"

"The soul."

"Sometimes. Other times, I don't know."

"That job of yours," she said. "All those crazy people. The criminals. It must be hard."

She fell silent for a while. Her body was tight against mine. We were moving toward a deeper, more convulsive rhythm.

I pulled up and glanced down into her face. She wrapped her legs around my haunches. Then suddenly, she laughed. It was a deep laugh, from a deep place, sleepy and provocative. She was in some ways a reckless woman.

I pulled away.

Out the window, there were low clouds coming down the hill. White clouds, fog really, and before too long that fog would come rushing down. The wind had already begun to nag at the rooftops. I was familiar with that nagging breeze—it hounded my house, mine and Elizabeth's, on the other side of the point, over in Golden Hinde.

"What's the matter?" she asked.

"Nothing. Let's slow things down. Make the time last."

The room held a vivid luminosity. The curtains, Sara's toes, her blouse draped over the chair—all were etched with light, an aura not unlike that which precedes certain types of seizures. It was often there for me at such moments, like the glow of the sun after it slips over the edge of the world. Entranced, though, lost in the moment, I sometimes did not recognize its presence until afterwards, in memory, so I cannot be sure even now, as I write this down, if it was there at all.

Sara rolled toward me. "We've been meeting like this for a while now," she said.

"Not so long. A few weeks."

"It wasn't what I had planned, you know. This kind of thing, with a married man. I have a boyfriend."

"I know."

"He wants to get serious with me."

"You told me that, yes."

"So what are we going to do?"

"I have to go over to the Correctional Facility this afternoon."

"That's not what I mean."

She was astride me now, and I reached up to touch her breasts. She yawned. The drink catching up with her. It was a strong drink—I knew how to mix them—and she'd taken it down pretty fast. My tie hung over her neck, draped like a scarf.

"Your wife, Elizabeth, she knows, doesn't she?"

"I don't think so."

"She will. Sooner or later."

I said nothing.

"So, what are you going to do? About us?"

Maybe that was the trigger. Sara's question. The anxiety it produced. I was confused, torn between two women. I still loved my wife. Or maybe it was simply something gone wrong in the soft mass of the brain. Something induced by the way she moved, eyes closed, straddling me—a kind of sleepy, drowsy, circling motion, as if she were slipping into a vortex and I was at its center. She didn't speak. Her head slumped and rolled back a little.

What happened next, exactly, it's hard to describe. I remember lying on my back, with Sara straddled over me. My grip was easy one instant, my hands gentle on her shoulders, then my grip tightened. I felt her resist, I saw her panic. My muscles were paralyzed, locked, and I could not open my hands to let her loose. I felt the convulsion. I lifted my head, looking into her eyes, trying to speak her name, but then she pulled away. I tugged back. I was clumsy and our heads butted, one against the other. Then I must've gone into a full fit. I went black. For how long, I'm not sure. I came back slowly, still in darkness. I could sense her movement in the room, hear her talking, but I could not move, and then the spell was broken and I was up, sitting on the edge of the bed. (I closed my eyes and saw a shadow inside myself, a little man moving within the shadow of another little man moving along the edge of a dark plane.) Sara stood across the room, bare-chested, holding the phone in her hands. She still wore her gray office skirt, hiked and rumpled. Her lip was bruised, badly, and my nose was bleeding.

"What happened?" She kept her distance, but her look was as much puzzlement as fear.

I tried to speak, but I couldn't. After such incidents, it takes a while to get back your tongue.

"Are you all right?"

I nodded.

"You really scared me."

Outside I heard a siren. An ambulance on its way up the hill.

"I called emergency," she said.

In another minute, the paramedics stood at the door, knocking. My voice returned, audible but faint. A kind of croaking. "I guess you better let them in," I said.

Sara grabbed a robe, something silk with a lace fringe. Held it close at the collar. I grabbed my pants from the floor.

She let the paramedics in. The first was tall and earnest, a bit breathless from the stairs. The second was a skinny little brute who looked as if he belonged on morgue detail. They took the scene in, glancing from one of us to the other.

The skinny one regarded me suspiciously. He turned to Sara. "Is this some kind of domestic squabble," he said. "Do we need a cop out here?"

"No," I insisted.

Then I staggered through an explanation. How as a kid I'd suffered from Hayes Syndrome. Or Blackout Syndrome, as it is more commonly known. Sudden fits—not seizures exactly, but something close. The child goes suddenly still, holding his breath, eyes open. Sometimes, the incidents go on for an inordinate amount of time, the skin turning blue, the veins bulging. Ultimately, they are not serious. They pass on their own. The biggest danger comes from the onlooker, the inclination to panic, to shake the victim: to force breath back into the body. This is exactly the wrong thing to do. Because the victim will thrash and rage, all the while unseeing, unconscious.

Usually Hayes Syndrome fades with time, though it has been known to linger through adolescence, even into adulthood, reappearing at times of emotional stress. I explained this all to the paramedics. I did not say, though, how there are other specialists who insist it is not a syndrome at all but rather an excuse—a pretense developed after the fact, as explanation for violent behavior of which the perpetrator is fully aware.

"I suffered an attack," I told the ambulance driver. "Sara

didn't know what to do. She tried to restrain me—and I guess we must have smashed heads."

The paramedic turned to Sara. "Is that what happened?"

Sara rubbed her wrists where I had grabbed her. She looked pretty shaken. I was embarrassed. I am not a violent man, I wanted to tell them, but I held my tongue, knowing the situation appeared otherwise—and the more I protested, the more they might disbelieve.

"He's telling the truth," she said at last. "I saw his body seize up. "

The driver had wandered into the kitchen. He came back with the empty vodka glass in his hand. He sniffed it.

"You two been drinking."

"No," said Sara. "I mean Jake had a drink. One. But I didn't have a drop."

I looked at her in surprise.

"I poured it down the sink," she explained.

I nodded but felt betrayed somehow. I remembered how she'd looked in bed above me—full of torpor, sleepy-eyed, as if on the edge of tumbling into a deep languor—but when I'd grabbed her shoulders, she'd jerked up pretty fast. Sober as a pin.

The skinny one took Sara aside now, going over the story with her in private. The other one helped me clean up my nose. He examined me a little bit, shining a light in my eyes, taking my pulse, my blood pressure. "It might be a good idea to come down to the hospital with us. Get an emergency CAT scan. Test things out."

The skinny one came back. He shrugged unhappily, as if disappointed Sara had not changed her story. They loitered around for a while, trying to persuade me into going to the hospital. I refused.

When they had gone, Sara sat beside me on the bed. The wariness was still there but mixed with something else. Concern, maybe. Compassion. She put her hand on my hand, and I felt the confusion well up once again.

"I'm sorry," I said. "Maybe. . . ." I stammered, looking

for an explanation.

"What?"

"I don't know. I can't say. This situation, the way things are with you and me."

"What are you saying?"

"Maybe it's the case I'm working. Sometimes, these things, they get inside your head. They twist you around."

"You frightened me," she said softly.

I put my arm around her. She was still edgy, but she seemed comforted in my presence, in the slow return to normalcy.

"I'm sorry," I said again.

"There's something about you," she said, "I can't resist."

She laughed a little. Then she kissed me with more sweetness than you might expect. She stroked my hair in back, adjusting my ponytail, fiddling. I touched the back of her head, too, and stroked her, telling her again how beautiful she was, how she reminded me of a girl I'd seen once, in a field of flowers, in an elevator, in a barroom, somewhere, once upon a time. She was a sweet girl but there was another side of her, too. She liked the sense of danger, the darkness underneath. I tasted her lips. I pulled away. I looked around. The aura was gone from the room.

2.

My wife and I lived out on Golden Hinde, a narrow spit of land that extends into the bay halfway between Sausalito and San Quentin. It was about ten minutes off the freeway, down a road that snaked and wound between the wetlands on one side and the brown hills on the other. The back of the house was all glass—you could see the water, the egrets, the sailboats, and San Quentin, too, castle-like across the bay. On a nice day our spot was as balmy a place as you could want, but often as not the wind funneled down over the hills. It was a nagging, irritating breeze. All the more so because just a few blocks over the air hung still and warm, perfect as can be.

Later that afternoon I was scheduled to meet with Matthew Dillard, the accused murderer, but I stopped first out at Golden Hinde. I had gotten blood on my shirt and needed to change.

Elizabeth was out of town. She had gone down to New Orleans to an academic conference—to read a paper on Jung, defending him from the new group of psychologists taking over the field. Then she had gone up to Anders, just outside of Baton Rouge. It was an old town, all but disappeared from the map, everything swallowed by kudzu and bamboo. Everything except the graveyard, that is. It was maintained by a sugar refinery nearby. Her mother and father were buried in that graveyard, and Elizabeth had gone to pay her respects.

She was her father's girl, mostly; he was the one she grieved.

I checked the mail—and found an invitation to the Wilders' party: an upscale bash we went to every summer. I put it aside and checked the answering machine, but Elizabeth hadn't called. I studied her picture on the mantelpiece. In it, she wore a necklace her father had given her, a string of pearls.

My wife and I had met on a tennis court. She worked at a teacher's college. I'd liked her long legs and the blunt cut of her hair. She was several years older than myself, but I liked that, too. She was an elegant woman, recently divorced. We'd been married three years but things had become difficult lately.

My fault, no doubt. My obsession with my job. My infidelities. Venal attractions to status and material comfort.

We had marble in the entry and granite in the kitchen and a sauna on the deck. We had a slate fireplace and a bookshelf full of metaphysical texts. On the mantle was a statue of the

Laughing Buddha—a fat-bellied little man who smiled vora-
ciously and looked as if he had just devoured the world.

We had a hot tub where I soaked and meditated. From
there, I could see Mt. Tamalpais looming over the county.

I was feeling off-kilter. The incident at Sara's had left me
disoriented, but there were other things, too. I'd had affairs
before, but usually they were brief things, a handful of
encounters, a night here, there, building in intensity—then
over. I would cut it off. I would be faithful for a while, six
months, a year, then something would build inside me. This
time, with Sara, I was more reckless. Letting it stretch out.
Being seen. A risky thing. It made you wonder who you
were. I wanted something new in my life, I guess, a new
exhilaration—one of those moments when you feel the
world brush against you, fragile and ungainly—but at the
same time I didn't want to lose Elizabeth. A contradiction, I
know, unrealistic. Selfish. I couldn't help myself. I took off
my clothes now. I had to be out at the Correctional Facility
in just a little while, to interview Dillard. In the meantime I
stood naked in the front of the mirror, regarding myself.

There was a game I had used to play with my patients. I
called it Peel the Onion. The point of this game was self-dis-
covery, to take them deeper into the self. I would pose the
simple question *Who are you?* and the patient would have
to respond quickly, in just a few sentences, nothing more.
Then I would ask the question again, then again. The trick
was for each answer to be truthful yet different than the one
before. Lying was not allowed. And to work right, to penetrate to the fundamental core, the game had to be played
quickly, without reflection.

I looked at myself again. My face was a mask.

Who are you?

Jake Danser, born 37 years ago in Baltimore, Maryland.
Married twice, both times to older women. First marriage
fell apart when my wife discovered I was having an affair
with a younger woman. She was dead now, my ex-wife.
Drowned off the coast of Mexico.

I reached down for my pants, caught a glimpse of my face in the mirror. My penetrating eyes and high cheekbones. My ponytail, longish in back.

Who are you?

A boy raised by his mother. No dad. Mom worked here and there to support little Jake. A teacher's pet at school. Interested in psychology. Boy prodigy.

Who are you?

Idealist. Worked for five years after college counseling the mentally ill in Los Angeles County Department of Corrections. Listened in patience. Later started my own practice for bored women and delinquent teenagers in Santa Monica. After divorce, moved to Marin County to begin successful, visible career as forensic psychologist.

I continued dressing as I went through the drill. Unfaithful husband. Lover. Man of a million faces. I put on my shirt. I combed my hair. I straightened my tie, my suit collar.

Professional witness. Advocate for the criminally insane.

I smiled. I was dapper as hell in my outfit, I had to admit. Women liked looking at me, I knew this, and I liked looking back. I liked touching, too. But this guy in the mirror, he was just a shell, nothing more. If you got underneath, what would you find? A hundred Jakes, maybe, and inside those a hundred more—but if you cracked all those open, and peered, and peered some more. . . .

Who are you?

I felt myself staring into the blackness. In my mind's eye, on the mantle, the Laughing Buddha stared back. What did he see? I wondered. A tremor. The smallest quiver in the dark, emanating. I checked myself one last time in the mirror. Smiled. Wiped a black tear from my cheek. Then went out to the Correctional Facilities to do the profile on Mr. Dillard.

3.

Before I continue, I know there are people, familiar with my case, who will say I am not telling the whole story here. That I leave out important information. If so, it is only because it's difficult to divulge everything at once, to get out all the facts without somehow going astray. Still I admit, in regard to the Dillard case, I have not told you everything. It is true, for example, that I had some acquaintance with Angela Mori, the accused's wife. Our worlds intersected. A few days before her death, I'd run into her at a lawn party at a suburban estate in Ross. We had danced together, and in a lascivious moment she had pressed her stomach close to mine. Dillard had been just a few yards away, his back turned, dancing with another woman.

Now he sat in front of me in the underground jail at the Marin County Correctional Facility. It was a cold place, dug into the ground beneath the Civic Center, a low-sloping building of spires and paint-gilded porticos that crouched drunkenly into the San Rafael hills.

Dillard was a good-looking man in his early thirties. He had dark eyes and fine features and skin the color of faded copper. He wore his hair short-cropped. He had grown up in West Oakland near the shipyards, in one of the black neighborhoods under the old Nimitz Freeway. His father was Creole. The old man had run a jazz club out on San Pablo Avenue, and Dillard knew how to move back and forth across social lines. Otherwise, he would never have ended up with Angela.

At the moment, Dillard was not at his best. He had the uncomfortable, smutty look that people get when you put them in an orange prison suit.

I tended to like him anyway. It is another one of my flaws. I feel camaraderie with my patients despite their crimes, or perhaps because of them. Part of me empathizes, maybe, more than it should. Looking at him, I remembered dancing with his wife. Elizabeth had been there as well that night, off in the back. She was the one who'd given me entry to this world, but it was my world, too, these days: Sara and Elizabeth; the lawyers and shrinks of Marin County; the dead woman and the man in front of me. I was tied to them all, twisted together even here, now, in this cell.

"How are you?" I asked Dillard.

"I been better."

"I can imagine," I said. "It must be a little rough."

I started to explain to him why I was here, but he cut me off. "You can skip the explanation, Doc. I been through it already. The court-ordered shrink was out here, and I know the routine."

Shortly after the indictment came down, the court had ordered a psychiatrist to examine Dillard. It was not unusual in cases like this, and in a lot of ways my examination would duplicate what had already been done. There was a difference though. The court psychiatrist had been merely looking to determine mental competence. My job was to gather evidence that might be useful in helping the defense attorney gain acquittal, or at least mitigate the sentence.

Dillard and I spent some time then going over his childhood, but I didn't really learn much that hadn't been established in the earlier report. I could see Dillard had a natural volatility and maybe some problems with impulse control. Even so, my original impressions were in line with those of the court psychiatrist. Just listening, off the top, nothing suggested the man was delusional.

"You went out with some buddies, the night Angela was killed?" I kept my voice low and friendly, pleasant, down-to-earth as possible. I smiled and tilted my head, waiting. Such mannerisms are all but second nature with me, but there is always another part of me watching wryly, detached, as if regarding the interchange from somewhere outside.

I thought of Sara then, I'm not sure why. I saw her hovering over me back at the apartment, and I saw Elizabeth, too, watching me the way she does, with that half-smile of hers, that sleepy look, full of knowing.

"I went to the fights," he said. "That's right. But you already know that. It's been in the papers."

He put his face down into his hands. He had very long fingers and they splayed up over his forehead.

"She rescued you, didn't she? From that life you were living."

The question was over the line, I suppose, presumptive in a way a psychologist is not supposed to be, but I wanted to jog him, to get things started. My goal was to determine Dillard's psychological state on the night of the murder.

Dillard glared at me. "What do you mean by that? There was nothing wrong with the life I was living."

I'd hit a nerve, I guess. Tennis court gigolo, that was the word on Dillard. An opportunist lounging in the land of silver Mercedes and white skirts. I knew the tag, because it had been applied to myself when I'd first come up here from Southern California.

It was not completely fair. I have my weaknesses—an attraction to the surface of things, to the glitter and the glam—but I have spent my time in the stacks: amongst the yellowing papers and the fine print and the endless analyses endemic to my profession.

"I didn't mean anything," I said. "I have a wealthy wife myself—and I know the kind of things people say." I smiled again, trying to put us both on the same level. "It's just women, how they rescue us all, you know. Save us from our worst selves."

Dillard bit his lip. His hands shook. I was waiting for the moment when it all started to gush out. When he explained for me his real feelings, and what the hell had happened between him and Angela that night.

"Maybe we could start with the day before Angela died. Go through it slow."

Like everybody in Marin County, I already knew the timeline. That evening after dinner, Dillard had gone out with some friends to a boxing match at the civic center. Sometime after that—late Saturday evening—Angela Mori was strangled to death in her bed.

Dillard, though, did not return home that night. Or that's what he'd told the police the first time around. Instead he'd spent the evening by himself, out on the family boat: a small yacht the Moris kept in the Sausalito harbor. He hadn't come home until the next day, mid-morning. Her car was parked out front, but the bedroom door was locked. He'd had to force it open—and that's when he discovered her body.

That was the story Dillard told in his initial statement to the police. As it turned out, the story did not hold. A neighbor had seen Dillard leave the house around midnight. She'd seen him slam out of the house, agitated, and drive off in a small frenzy.

So the police had brought Dillard back in.

The second time around, he told it differently. He'd been back to the house, he admitted. Late that night, after the fights. About midnight, like the neighbor said. He found the bedroom door locked. He pounded on it, but Angela didn't answer. He pounded some more.

I'd read the transcripts, so I knew Dillard's explanation. He'd lied the first time out of fear, he told the police. Because he knew how it looked, him driving away from the house in the middle of the night. But the truth was he thought Angela was in there, giving him the silent treatment, locking him out, like she sometimes did.

So he drove away out of anger. He'd had no idea, he claimed, that Angela was lying dead on the other side of the door.

According to the coroner's report, Angela had been strangled with a tie from Dillard's wardrobe. The report indicated semen in her vagina, and foreign pubic hair had been found on her body and in the bed. The DNA report hadn't come back from the lab, but the hair analysis identified the pubic as belonging to Dillard. More incriminating, though, was the small spray of blood on a shirt the cops found in a hamper out on the family boat: the same shirt Dillard had been wearing the night of the murder.

The coroner's report had indicated something else, too. Angela had had a drink before she died, and the drink had been spiked with gamma hydroxybutrate. Gamma was a knock-out drug, otherwise known as Big G, or Liquid Ecstasy, or just X— a cousin to the stuff kids were taking over in the Haight, at their tie-dye dances. A lot of people liked it for its dopey, amorous high, but it also could put you under pretty hard, especially when mixed with alcohol.

"How were you getting along, you and Angela, you know, in terms of your marriage?"

"How you getting along in yours?"

I ignored the remark. It was the kind of thing you got sometimes, situations like this, from people who didn't like the questions; so they tried to bait you, to switch focus, dragging your personal life into the session. The boundaries were thin enough.

"You ever get jealous?"

"You didn't answer my question."

"This isn't about me. Did you ever get jealous?"

Dillard paused, then went ahead and answered. "Angela liked to flirt. It made me angry, sometimes, but I didn't kill her over it."

"You and Angela, you liked to drink."

"Sometimes."

"Drugs?"

"No."

"You used to do cocaine, didn't you?"

"So did everyone."

"Did you ever hear voices when you take drugs? You know what I mean?"

"You trying to see if I'm crazy?"

His lips tilted into a smile then, and his eyes fixed mine, and just for an instant I saw the charm in the man, the confident lilt and debonair carriage. Inappropriate under the circumstances. Evidence of psychopathic tendencies, maybe—that, and the way he'd tried to twist the conversation back my way—but I'd seen the same behavior plenty of times, in plenty of people, and not all of them were psychopaths. Not all psychopaths were murderers, either. Some were chronic liars. Womanizers. Run-of the mill thieves.

"Some people, they do drugs," I said, "it sets off part of their brain. They hear things, do things, they might not ordinarily. That ever happen to you?"

"No."

"That night, at dinner, you went to the Blue Chêz, in San Rafael?"

"Yes."

"What did you have to eat?"

"What kind of question is that?"

"I was just asking."

"My wife is dead, and you want to know whether I had the demi-glaze with pearled onions. . . . "

"I am just trying to see how your memory is."

"I had steak and she had some kind of fish."

"What did you talk about?"

"Angela's yacht, in Sausalito. It needs a new hull. Things like that. Domestic."

"Did you argue?"

"No. Not at all."

"What did you do when you got home?"

He didn't skip a beat. "We made love."

"You and Angela."

"Who else? We were the only ones in the house."

"How was it?"

"You ask some funny questions. How is it with your wife?"

"I just want to see how you were feeling. How it made you feel."

"It was fine," he said. His eyes were teary now. Genuine or not, I had no idea. Such moments can be hard to gauge even in yourself.

"Then what?"

"I got dressed and went out. I went to the fights, like I said."

"Did you do drugs?"

"I had a few beers. A couple shots."

"Anything else?"

He hesitated. "Smoked some pot. It was no big deal."

"Were you worked up, when the fight was over?"

"A little bit—it was a good fight."

"Your man lost?"

"Yeah. My guy lost."

I didn't say anything else for a while, and neither did he. My thoughts drifted to my own predicament, to Golden Hinde, the empty house, to Sara and Elizabeth, and the decision that lay waiting ahead. For an instant I felt caged, too, trapped. Such feelings came over me sometimes, in jail, interviewing clients—and I felt a quiver inside my chest: a desire to penetrate the world, and at the same time to smother that desire into nothing. I loved my wife, I told myself. Dillard glanced at me curiously. Our interview had turned into an interrogation. I preferred the conversation to go differently—for the subject to talk while I listened— but sometimes this was just how things went. You fell into a pattern.

"You'd been with a couple of your old friends. You'd been drinking and smoking dope. And then you . . . "

"I came home," he said, and then he told the same story, more or less, that he'd told the police the second time around, and the same story he'd told the other shrink as well. How he'd come inside the darkened apartment and taken a piss in the hall bathroom, then walked back to the bedroom to the locked door.

"I figured she locked me out. We'd had some words earlier, and I figured she was angry."

"I thought you said everything was okay."

"She'd pulled stuff like that, Angela. She was a bit of a case, sometimes."

"Then what happened."

"I went out to the boat. In the morning, when I came home—I was already to forget about it, just another day in the life—but the bedroom door was still locked. I got a screwdriver—and that's when I found her."

His lip quivered. I didn't know what to think. To believe Dillard's story, you had to believe someone else had visited his wife earlier that night. That the visitor had spiked his wife's drink. Raped her, murdered her, then locked the bedroom door behind him. Possible, certainly—but all the physical evidence pointed to Dillard. His tie around her neck. His fingerprints. His pubic hair in the bed. The spot of blood.

Then in the closet—inside his jacket pocket—the police had found something else: a vial of Liquid X. The same substance had been in Angela's blood the night she died.

"The blood on the shirt?" I asked.

It wasn't my job to ask questions about the evidence, of course. But I was curious how he would explain it. And the world of the psychological and the physical, they sometimes overlap.

"When we made love, after the restaurant. Her lip . . . " He stumbled over his words. "We got a little rough sometimes, you know, just playing around. Clumsy, really. My shoulder . . . " He shrugged. "Listen—if I killed her, if I used my tie, why would I leave it lying around like that? Or the shirt. Why wouldn't I toss it? I mean I'd have to be pretty stupid, wouldn't I?"

"Killers don't always behave rationally," I said. "In rage, another part of the brain takes over."

Even so there was some truth to what Dillard was saying. Most of the evidence against him was pretty much circumstantial. If it wasn't for his initial story, he might not even be in custody now. But the lie, it drew the prosecution. That—and the blood on his shirt.

Angela's blood, the police claimed. Aspirated up the through the lungs as she was dying, onto the lips.

The prosecution would say the blood had gotten on Dillard's shirt when he strangled her. But Dillard's explanation could just as well be true. She could have bitten her lip when he clumsied into her, heaving forward in a moment of passion.

I tried another tack: the kind of thing I did when I worked the other side of the fence, for the prosecution. If you could catch a subject off guard, antagonize them, sometimes they'd say something to let themselves show.

"She was a looker, though, I'll say that," I said.

"What do you mean?"

"Angela. I knew a girl like her once. A lot like her."

He glinted up at me, full of suspicion. It was a nasty trick, but it was part of my job.

"Some of these women, sometimes," I said, "you have to show them. You know what I mean?"

"No."

"Give them the back of the hand. A little taste. And if things get carried away. . . ."

He smiled for a second, and I thought I had him. He was going to say something. Let the truth loose with a wink and nod. We were compadres. We knew how to treat women. I gave him an awkward grin, an awful person in league with another awful person. He saw through me then, I think. I was not the person I pretended.

He shook his head.

"Can the shit, Doc." He looked into my eyes. "I'm innocent on this. I came home and I found her body. That's the truth of it. I'm not going to play nut for you. That's what my lawyer wants, but I'm being framed up on this, that's the truth of it. I'm being goddamned framed."

Afterwards, I went to the gym on Marsh Road. I put in maybe an hour on the weights, pumping iron. I liked to be methodical about my workouts, to go from station to station, machine to machine, working until my shirt was damp with perspiration and my muscles gave out. Meanwhile I watched the women in their shining spandex, the fading beauties of Marin County. Doctor's wives. Yoga teachers. Poetesses. The dilettantes and artistes. I had a certain affection for them. We had something in common. An unfulfilled moment, an instant waiting to happen.

I left the gym, but there was something brooding in me.

At such times, I would go down to my trailer—down off Lucky Drive, at the edge of the Corte Madera marsh—and that's where I went now. My fishing trailer, I called it, though in fact I'm not much of an angler. I'd driven it up here from Los Angeles, and I'd lived there for almost a year before I met Elizabeth, while I got my new practice off the ground. It was at the end of a gravel road, just beyond the trailer court. I had some files there—overflow from my office—but more than that it was a place I went sometimes to contemplate. I could see San Quentin from here, too, from the front steps of the trailer. The sun was going down, disappearing behind Mt. Tamalpais, and the bay waters in front of the prison shimmered a brilliant red. Then the wind drove me inside and I lay down on the bunk.

I had pictures here. Clippings. A strong box full of mementos. I kept the metal box in a drawer and I opened it now. Nothing really. Just bits of cloth and paper and tinsel. Even so, it was a connection to my past. Things I had done and people I had known.

Outside night descended over the water.

Sara, I thought.

I saw her face. Other women I have known. All their faces tumbling into the darkness. I shut the box.

What do people really know of themselves? I wondered.

I sat for a while in the lotus position but it did not change my feeling. I was still restless.

I called Golden Hinde to check my messages, but there was nothing. I got in the Audi, still not knowing what I meant to do. I felt a black desire, I confess, a certain need.

Rooted in the body chemistry, in the old hunter instincts, maybe, or metaphysical despair, I don't know. I wanted Elizabeth then, I told myself, but she was far away. I thought I might go see Sara, but the way things had gone last time, it made me hesitant. I headed down 101 but I did not take the Sausalito exit. Instead I headed over the grade toward the city—catching a glimpse of the bridge from high ground, then the peninsula beyond with its financial towers, its pyramid, its hills—all glittering like Oz across the dark water. I drove into SOMA then, to the club district. I drank in the DNA lounge for a while, then went to another place around the corner. It was Friday, and the bridge-and-tunnelers were out mingling with the city types, though you couldn't tell the difference. Techies and new wave hipsters. Women in black. They smoked thin cigars and drank and posed like decadent bourgeoisie on a Parisian boulevard. They had ugly faces and beautiful faces smeared with cosmetics and white faces as innocent as the moon and tired faces that glistened with the first blush of alcohol after a long week of tending computer screens and dreaming of secret encounters in places like this.

Inside the dancing and lights could get pretty vicious. I needed a little bit of escape, a way out of myself. Out on the floor, I met a girl in a loose-fitting dress who had a sheen on her face and threw her arms out wildly as she danced. I didn't ask her name. We got lost in the moment.

Then, across the room, I saw a man I recognized, one of those people you meet in my line of work but you don't really want to see on the street. An extortion artist. Accused murderer. His name was Tony Grazzioni, and I'd interviewed him once, in a professional capacity, down in the San Bernardino County Jail.

I turned back to the girl then and pulled her toward me. We got a little wilder. She had brown hair and hazel eyes, and she wore a green shift that stopped at mid-thigh and also black jet beads that swung about her neck. Given the way she hugged and thrust, and her dreamy eyes, I guessed she was on ecstasy or one of its variants: MDMA, or gamma, or good old-fashioned chloral. They were all popular in the clubs here. We did the bump and grind, and drank, and I began to feel high, higher than I should, and libidinous, and I began to think maybe she had spiked my drink, because that was the kind of thing people were doing then, casual acquaintances who worried you might otherwise find them a bit drab. I went to the bar to get us a couple more drinks.

A voice came at me from behind. A hand nudged my shoulder.

"Hi, doc, remember me?"

"No," I said.

I was lying. I knew who it was, even before I turned and looked. I'd recognized the high-throated voice. Tony Grazzioni.

Back when I knew him, he'd been charged with murder. A for-hire job. Involving an oil executive's wife, and a coat hanger tightened with baling pliers about the neck.

He put his face close to mine. He was a big man, with a big face, acne-scarred, ugly like a dog. He wore a cologne that smelled like the inside of a roadside motel.

"I see you're working the scene—again," he said. "Nice looking girl."

"Go fuck yourself, Tony."

After he'd been acquitted, Grazzioni had made a clumsy effort at blackmailing me, based on some things I'd told him in a psychiatric session. It was a professional hazard, running into guys like Grazzioni, and sometimes the only way to handle it was to just walk off. I searched out the girl. We drank our drinks and danced some more. Grazzioni didn't leave right away. He hung around at the back of the bar watching us dance. There was another man beside him, a small-time dealer who was somewhat of a fixture around here. I'd seen him a number of times. A pale wallflower in a black nylon shirt and dark khakis who peddled his wares from club to club, and liked to lean back and watch his clients out on the floor.

He and Grazzioni started to talk, and I saw Grazzioni gesture at me, and the dealer said something else.

I didn't like this.

I'd been here before in this same club, dancing, and I didn't like the way the guy was leaning over, talking to Tony, and I didn't like that grin on Tony's face.

It began to feel like one of those fateful moves, my decision to come here, one of those wrong turns you didn't think anything about at the time but later came back to haunt you.

I steered the girl away from them and out the door. I tried to put Grazzioni out of my mind. The girl and I ended up in a loft apartment nearby, thumping hard against one another's glistening bodies. I was pretty high by this time, and felt as if we were on the edge of some precipice, myself and the girl together, with the darkness way down below. We went after it long and hard, and for an instant I was outside myself, watching, looking into the girl's face and watching myself from above at the same time, or so it felt, waiting for the moment when I would fall through my reflection, through the blackness at the center of her eyes. Then I remembered Grazzioni, peering at me from across the room. The girl went over the edge, moaning and panting, but I stayed where I was. I tried to follow her but it was no good. Grazzioni had ruined my evening.

4.

What can I say to redeem myself? Should I tell you how I rolled over in bed next to that girl and yearned for my wife? How just looking at her filled me with a loneliness I can't describe? I felt locked out. Filled with disappointment, self-disgust. I gave the girl a kiss—a tender kiss, sweet and full of self-loathing—but she was all but asleep now and none of it meant anything. I drove over the bridge to my empty house and slid into the hot tub, all alone, trying to wash those emotions clean. I sipped a glass of wine there in the swirling waters, staring meanwhile at the prison across the bay, but the feelings didn't wash off.

I settled deeper into the water, the jets lapping against me. For a minute I was a man within a man within the void, and it was the void that imagined me, I told myself.

But when I opened my eyes, I was still there, flesh and blood, locked in the moment, tormented by unacceptable passions. The mountain loomed over me in the dark. The Sleeping Maiden, the Indians had called Mt. Tamalpais. A child of the heavens, they said, who dreamed the world into existence as she slept. I raised my glass to her looming shadow. Then I finished my wine and went to bed.

5.

Two days later, Elizabeth came home. She was a lean woman, elegant, with a pale complexion and very blue eyes. When I first met her, not much more than three years ago now, her hair had still been black, with undertones of gray, platinum really, that she made no effort to hide. She'd worn it mussed, and the effect was that of sophisticated, reckless descent into age. Now the balance had changed, and the platinum was dominant. The black and the gray were undertones, carefully controlled by her colorist, of course, but the effect overall was striking. She had the look of blue smoke, of white ice so cold it was hot to the touch. She had just turned forty-four but in a room with other women, a lot of eyes, even those of the younger men, were drawn to her.

She stood looking through the mail. She wore, as almost always, the pearl necklace her father had given her.

I went up behind her now, encircled her waist with my arms. I felt her resistance but also the give in her body, the pleasure. Her fingers toyed with the Wilders' invitation.

"The party's not for weeks, it says. Why do they send it so early?"

"So everyone can make their plans, I guess."

"No," she said. "It's because they want their party to dominate the summer. The event of the season. You know how they are."

"Barbara Wilder has always been nice to me."

"That's because you're a man."

She put the invitation aside.

"Have you eaten?" I asked.

"Not yet."

"Let's go out then."

"Let me change first."

"You don't have to change. You look fine."

"No," she insisted. "Just give me a minute."

I walked out to the car to get her luggage. I dallied for a while. Outside the weather was idyllic. The air hung utterly still and the light danced in a breathless way across the grass, giving you the sensation of something just out of reach. Elizabeth and I met on the tennis court, as I may have mentioned. She was a divorcée, good looking, self-sufficient. In those early days, we would talk about depth psychology. About Freud and Jung and Otto Rank. About the attraction of opposites, the yin and the yang. About the exploration of the darkness and the individuation of the soul.

I glanced around at the house, and all that we had, and at the picture of us, just married, that hung on the wall.

A good-looking couple, people said about us. Or so I imagined.

Swank.

Professional people with intelligence and ambition.

Maybe not so much intelligence, though, at least not on my part. Otherwise I would not risk our future the way I did. I could blame my childhood, I suppose. Or Elizabeth. Or the pace of modern living, as the magazines liked to say. I could blame the television, too, and cell phones, and methyl chloride in the bay. The truth was, there were patterns in people's lives, things that happened over and over. I'd seen it in the people I treated, in the criminals as well as the normal folks, so-called. Little changed those patterns. They were like waveforms, the fundamental energy of the person.

Inside I found Elizabeth in the den, on the phone. Her blouse was untucked. She stood with her back to me, very still. She laughed more lustily than usual. Then something all but imperceptible changed in her stance. She had sensed my presence.

She got off the phone.

"Who was that?"

"Fran."

Fran was an old friend of hers, a loud and busty woman with whom she'd had a falling out some time back. They were competitive, the two of them, and I was surprised to hear them back in touch.

"What's she up to?"

"Not much. She wants to get together and tell me about her newest fling."

"I thought you were angry with her."

"Not so much."

Elizabeth smiled but I sensed her aloofness and felt again the confusing emotions that dominated our marriage lately. I would want her, then I wouldn't. My feelings were complicated. Desire intermingled with flashes of anger—and the sense of something about to end.

I watched her change clothes. Something more demure—black slacks and a gray blouse, open at the collar—but she kept the pearls.

"How was the conference?" I asked.

"Not so bad."

"No bloody noses? Fights in the parking lots?"

"Not this time."

In the old days, it had been the Jungians against the Freudians, and both sides against the followers of B. F. Skinner. Those who saw personality rooted in the soul against those who believed it was a matter of social conditioning. Nowadays they had all fallen to the background and the field was dominated by researchers and statisticians—in short, by the genetic determinists—who believed everything we did, who we are, how we behaved, was all determined by biochemistry, which in turn had its roots in the genetic code.

"So they've discovered civility."

"Yes."

"That's a shame."

I was trying to be funny, the way we were with each other sometimes, frothy and tart.

"It's a bit of a relief, really," she said.

"I understand, but it spoils our conversation. I used to enjoy hearing about them. At each other's throats."

"Actually, the field is moving towards a consolidation of ideas. It's an exciting time." She enjoyed her work and was not in the mood, at least at the moment, to mock her colleagues.

"How's the Dillard case going?" she asked.

"It's too soon to know."

"Who's handling the prosecution?"

"Minor Robinson."

"Oh, yes, Minor."

I watched her face in the mirror. She kept expressionless, pretty much. Minor was a widower. He had moved here from LA about the same time as myself, but he'd met Elizabeth sooner, and the two of them had gone out for a while. I'd seen them playing tennis a couple of times before Elizabeth and I had gotten together. He'd been my rival, I guess, though how much spark there'd been between them, I didn't know. I did know that Minor wasn't fond of me. Since he'd been promoted to lead prosecutor, my referrals from the county had dropped off. Almost all my clients were on the defense side now.

"How's Minor doing?" she asked.

"He's doing fine. I ran into him at the courthouse last week."

"I saw him myself, a couple of weeks back," she said. "In Larkspur—at the racquet club. I was waiting for Fran."

"Oh."

She turned to me now. The gray in the blouse brought out the gray in her hair, but the effect was not unattractive. Her eyes were an icy blue. Something about the way she looked at me, it went right through me.

"Where do you want to go to dinner?"

"The Blue Chêz."

It was a place we went often. So did a lot of other people we knew, particularly in the legal profession. It was an upscale restaurant in the so-called French Quarter up in San Rafael. It had been a larger neighborhood once, I think, but it was hard to tell because now it stood isolated under the downtown underpass, a block or so of plankboard Victorians done over in muted colors, with bright flowers in the boxes outside.

It was also, as I have mentioned, the place Dillard took his wife the evening she was murdered.

A valet took our car. On the restaurant walls hung paintings of the French countryside. In those pictures blowzy women swung baskets of cheese and bread down cobbled alleys. The alleys were clean and bright, with no sign of menace.

We made small talk.

The waitress brought the first course, asparagus and walnuts in a fruit vinaigrette.

We ordered a Chardonnay from the Alexander Valley.

The room bubbled, and fragments of conversation from the surrounding tables drifted through our first course. I experienced one of those moments when the boundaries between myself and the world seemed less pronounced than usual, as if the snippets of talk originated from within myself. *I've been reading Thomas Moore, you know, his book about the nature of the soul.* A Mexican waiter refilled our glasses, head bent. High-throated laughter echoed from somewhere nearby, disembodied. *The baby boomers are inheriting everything, but they don't deserve it. It's their parents did all the work.* My thoughts were filtered through the wine, part of the conversation around me. Elizabeth's gaze was on the table, focused inward. *Have you been following the Mori case? She was a bit of a run-around from what I hear.*

The waiter returned

More Chardonnay. Same vintage. With a taste of oak and not too fruity.

Never mind the price.

It was a weeknight, and before long the Courthouse Gang arrived, as they called themselves, and they took a table by the window. I had been a member of the group myself once. Among them were Minor Robinson and also Alex Milofski, the homicide cop.

After a while, Minor came over to our table.

"Elizabeth, Jake," he said, nodding to each of us in turn. "How are you doing?"

"Wonderful," I said. "Just wonderful."

He was a good-looking man about my age, lean and well built, with black hair and a spike of gray at the temple. People said we looked alike but any resemblance was pretty superficial. He had a certain warmth, it was true, a wholesomeness that women liked—but there was also something about him that was a little too crisp, too earnest, for my taste anyway, a kind of FBI officiousness, a moral sensibility, a confidence in what is right, what is wrong, that got under my skin.

Elizabeth smiled.

"How was your trip to Louisiana?" he asked.

"Fine." Elizabeth lowered her eyes and I thought about the two of them out on the tennis court.

"Would you like to join us?" I asked.

"No, no. I heard you were working with Haney Wagoner on the Dillard case. So I thought I'd come over and give you a friendly, adversarial hello."

"Well, hello, then," I said. "This place is pretty busy for a Monday night."

"It's been busier since the murder, I understand," said

Elizabeth. There was a small gleam in her eye. "They ate here that night, didn't they?"

"Sure," I said. "A little murder, it's good for business."

"Yes. But Dillard didn't kill her here," said Minor.

"Maybe he didn't kill her at all," I offered.

"Come on. There's not much doubt about that. Otherwise, why's Haney lining up his psychiatric experts? You examined him yet?"

"Can't talk about that."

"No?"

"You'll have to ask Haney. If he goes with the psychological defense, I'm sure you guys will get your shot."

It was the kind of case, a couple of years back, I would have been testifying as a prosecution witness myself, gathered around the table with the rest of them, drinking and joking. Things had changed, though, since Minor's promotion—and I was on the outside now.

Finally Minor left us and went back to his table. I couldn't say I was sorry to see him go.

Elizabeth raised her glass to her lips.

"He sounds confident."

"Well, he's got a good case. And Angela's coffin—it makes a great stepping stone."

"You sound bitter."

"I'm not. You know that, hon. I've got everything."

I leaned over and smiled as well as I could. She was skeptical but she couldn't help herself, she smiled back. I put my hand on her hand, and listened to her talk about her father, her home, and as she did her accent thickened, the Southern voice, central Louisiana, no longer the drawl with the edges taken off—softened by a few years out east and another dozen in California—but the younger voice, raw and melodic, the sound of the swamp and petticoats and the radio over the water on a humid night, the kind of voice men hear in their dreams as they drift off to sleep on the long drive over Lake Pontchartrain. Her accent always thickened as she talked about home, and I was seduced into seeing myself as part of that world, in that old house, walking in her father's shadow.

By the time we finished dinner, the Courthouse Gang had left. It didn't matter, I knew I'd see them again soon, like it or not. If not in the courtroom, then at the Wilders' party, in the not too distant future. The Wilders had a fondness for forensic types, particularly those involved in the psychological end of things.

We drove back through the dark along Marsh Road. We wound away from Highway 101, following the bay, snaking along the low ridge between the marsh and the high brown hills. On occasion, you could see the prison, glistening across the inlet. Houses lay in the hollows below us, on the shore between the bay and the road.

"How did Minor know you were in Louisiana?"

"I must have mentioned it to him. Didn't I tell you? I ran into him at the racquet club."

"Oh. I didn't realize you had spoken."

"We talked—for a little while. He's a bright man."

"In a pedestrian kind of way."

She laughed. "That's not nice."

"I'm not trying to be nice."

We pulled into the driveway. I put my hand on her leg, and kissed her. Her lips were wet and cool, but her response was abstract, far away. Still, she excited me. I touched the collar of her expensive blouse, kissed her again and tasted the drawl in her mouth.

"I'm so tired. It was a long trip."

"Don't worry. I'll let you be."

We went inside. Despite what I said, I wanted to reach for her. I watched her take off her blouse. She had a black bra on underneath. I watched her take off that, too, and then she slipped away from me, into the tub, and shut the door behind her.

Elizabeth was a glamorous woman in many ways, sophisticated in her manner and her ideas. In some ways, though, she'd never gotten over her first divorce. Her first husband had been a writer—an alcoholic, a womanizer—and the break-up had come not long after her father's death. She was vulnerable when she met me, not long divorced. We'd driven down to Stinson Beach, on the other side of Mt. Tamalpais. I'd been quiet and shy and kept my hands to myself. A bit of an act, though there are times, around certain women, that I feel this way. I'd studied her age lines, the fine web about her eyes, and smelled her cosmetics, the silk blouse faint with sweat. We'd sat in the open convertible beneath the Monterey Pines in sight of the ocean. I'd been pursuing her and she'd been pursuing me, and people were talking, we both knew this. I'd liked her convertible, I admit, and her father's money. In the end it wasn't those things, no. There were other women with those things.

It was the smell of her maybe. Something in her eyes, at once vulnerable and haughty, a glance that cut to the quick, full of presentiment, a suggestion there was something waiting ahead for us.

We kissed. I touched her all over.

If I could have lost myself inside her then, that moment at the beach, if I could have crawled inside her and disappeared, I would have done so.

Who am I?

I yearned now to be one of my other selves. One of those other Jakes. The earnest psychologist, perhaps, in love with his college teacher wife. The faithful husband.

I went away from Elizabeth into the living room. The little Buddha was there, with his mouth twisted into a smile. I found a copy of the *Examiner* and went through it. There was a story about Angela Mori. Details about the murder. There was more on the inside page. Information unearthed by the defense and leaked out to reporters. Angela's sex life, the many men she had slept with; rumors, unsubstantiated, about secret liaisons in a hotel in Novato. An unidentified man—a man in a blue suit, the paper said. A search of the hotel records turned up nothing. The story made me uneasy.

Angela was reckless, it was true. I remembered how she'd leaned against me and put her tongue in my ear. There were always rumors about a girl like that. There was even one rumor—a joke, really, muttered in the courthouse halls—tying her to Minor Robinson.

No one believed it, though. He was too concerned with his image to risk himself like that. Too much the prig.

I laughed thinking about it, clutching the newspaper in my hand, a laugh that was a bit forced, I realize now, clumsy and awkward, though I wouldn't have admitted it at the time.

I didn't hear Elizabeth finish her bath. When I went into the bedroom, the lights were out, and she was on the edge of sleep. I put my arm around her. She was in her pajamas, white silk. She moaned softly in the dark, and I lay a little while like that, thinking about Angela Mori and also about Sara and the episode from a few days before. Lying in the dark as I was now—inside our house, on this narrow point of land, extending into the bay—it seemed to me for a moment that everything else in the world was nothing but a dream, all the events of the world, the news, the daily buzz. There was in reality nothing but this dark, and all else was illusion. I put my hand up over Elizabeth's breast, on the outside of her pajamas, and pushed myself against her from behind. "No," she moaned, "Honey, no," and I pushed a little harder, feeling for the opening between the buttons in her blouse, touching her nipple, the aureole. She lay on her side, her back to me, and I cradled her buttocks with my free hand, and then I slid down the pajama bottoms "No, honey, please. . . ." she said again, but that was all. She was on her stomach now. Her face was in the pillow. She began to breathe more heavily, panting more deeply. Not quite voluntary. I reached lower, between her legs. I spread her buttocks. "No," she said, her fingers reaching, "no." I pushed harder. She gasped as I entered from behind.

PART TWO

The Decision

6.

I know, of course, the latest research suggesting evil originates in a particular part of the brain. Near the hippocampus, some say, beneath the memory center, in the old lizard part of the mind. In a neurological space where everything we pretend to be, all our mores, disappear like stray thoughts into the abyss. Where the whisperings of the neocortex no longer matter and the blood impulses take over.

But how does this happen? By what mechanisms? Under which conditions?

Such questions are at the heart of every criminal case, I suspect, if not everything we do, and they were on my mind then, as I went once again to the Correctional Facility, to the little room with the plastic chairs and the panic button on the wall.

I enjoyed my work. Though my role was a subversive one in many ways, and there were quite a few who did not like me—the prosecutors, the cops, the jailers—I enjoyed it nonetheless. Like all work, it was a form of self-exploration, but at the same time it gave me refuge from my self, and refuge, too, from my personal life, from certain things looming on the horizon of which I was aware—but there was a part of me (as there often is, I suppose) that did not want to acknowledge such concerns.

I had to make a stand sooner or later, if only with myself, but I was not ready for that yet. So I immersed myself in my work.

I had been called to the jail by Dillard's lawyer, Haney Wagoner, a congenial-seeming man with oversized eyebrows whose wife was friends with Elizabeth. Elizabeth had introduced us, and though I had qualifications of my own—and experience as well—that introduction had helped get me the case. Wagoner was fond of Elizabeth, and asked after her wistfully, as men often did.

"She's fine," I said. "Absolutely wonderful."

"Good, good. We used to see more of her, in the old days."

"She misses you both," I said, though in fact she seldom mentioned either of them unless it was in regard to their increasing girth. "I'm afraid we all used to get together more often, in the old days."

"Yes, we used to see her quite a bit. When she was married to David. Not that it was a good marriage. No, no." He leaned toward me confidentially, arching those large brows of his. "He had a charming manner, her first husband. He was the kind of guy you like to be around. At first. But there was a darkness underneath. I was glad to see him go."

"Me, too." I joked, though in fact I had never met him.

He laughed, and so did I, but there was awkwardness between us, something stiff and uneasy. Wagoner was in his early fifties and had a reputation among the public on account of a celebrity he'd helped acquit some twenty years before. Among his peers he was not so well regarded. He had a one-track mentality, people said, and his office was poorly run. I didn't know if these things were true. Though my own dealings with him had been cordial enough, and his manner suggested he knew his business, it soon became apparent he was having trouble with his client.

"I don't want to do my defense this way," said Dillard. "I didn't kill her. I didn't do it."

Wagoner wore a vest with a white shirt beneath, open at the collar, and no tie. He took off his vest, getting down to business, and sat across from his client. He seemed agitated, as if he had been at this for a while. "If we don't convince the jury there were extenuating circumstances," he told Dillard, "they'll give you the death penalty."

Dillard looked smaller since that last time I'd seen him, worn down by his time in the stir.

"I didn't kill her," he insisted.

Haney turned to me then, drawing me into the conversation. "Dr. Danser," he said. "You're familiar with the kind of tricks the mind can play on itself, in traumatic situations. You know the term. Anxiety-induced situational memory loss." Haney spoke the phrase with a certain flourish, as if it held the key to his case.

I knew the term. It was from Rudolf Kleindst, the man who wrote the book on memory blackout. It was a subject in which I found myself involved on occasion—partly, I suppose, because my own clinical history had prompted an interest in the subject. My interest was natural enough. People who suffer certain conditions tend to study them with a passion others might not possess. So I had some expertise.

In the medical community, selective amnesia has long been known to accompany certain sorts of physical injuries and convulsive fits. The idea that such amnesia might accompany emotional trauma—this was a cloudier subject. Murkier still was the notion that suppressed memories of violence could spur violence by the victim himself, and this violence, too, would go unremembered. It was controversial stuff, but Kleindst's forays into the subject had been enjoying a renaissance in the popular imagination lately, spurred by the media.

"You're the expert," said Haney. "Explain this syndrome to my client here, this psychological condition. Explain it so a regular person can understand."

What Haney wanted to do, I realized, was coach his client: to prepare him to testify in such a way as to support the alleged mental condition. I had my doubts as to whether all the markers were there in regard to Dillard. Also I'd been following the case, and I knew that some irregularities had emerged regarding the hard evidence, particularly the DNA. One of the samples had been contaminated. Most attorneys would go after that flaw in the evidence. They would pull at it, then pull some more, doing what they could to unravel the prosecution's case. In contrast, Haney remained focused on the psychological.

It was a risky strategy, the kind that had worked a decade before, when the insanity defense was popular. Now juries were different—and so were the laws.

Looking back, I tell myself I should have been more forceful about my reservations, but I knew Haney had enlisted a number of well-known psychologists as expert witnesses. Among them was Madison Paulie, who'd made his reputation profiling serial killers. Those of you who work in the profession will recognize his name: a specialist in criminal deviancy, known for his objectivity, one of the few who worked both sides of the aisle, prosecution and defense, and had the respect of both. He'd taken the stand on behalf of the Vampire Killer, over in Sacramento, pleading for clemency, but he'd also testified against the Chinatown Rapist, laying out the accused's irremediable psychopathy in no uncertain terms. I had met Paulie once in passing—at one of the Wilders' parties, as it happened—and it appealed to my vanity, I confess, to be part of a top-flight team. I was flattered.

"This kind of syndrome," I said, "the one you're talking about—the victims block out memories of their abuse. Things that happened to them in the past. Violent things. Unpleasant things. They block out those memories. And they block out their own abusive actions."

Wagoner turned once again to Dillard. The prisoner looked bewildered. The case was moving away from him—and away, too, from whatever had or had not happened that night between him and Angela.

"Did your father ever abuse you?" asked Wagoner.

"No."

"Did he ever hit you—you know, with a strap, or a belt?"

"Not that I remember."

Wagoner ignored the answer and returned his attention to me. "If Dillard suffered from this kind of memory loss, in regard to his father beating him, how would this affect his memory of those events."

"Well, any number of ways," I said. "He could remember some of the incidents but not others. He might remember them to a certain point—say to when the beatings started to get intense. Or maybe the whole incident would float somewhere in the back of his head, and seem more like a dream than a memory. He could see his father looming over him. . . ."

"Please," Dillard interrupted. "My father was a good man."

Haney sighed and shook his head. He knitted those unwieldy eyebrows together—they were a natural calamity of sorts, those eyebrows, thick and black, a line of charcoal across his brow—and his face furrowed. "Let's approach this from another angle. You told me you had a special relationship with your Aunt Florence. You carry a picture of her in your wallet, don't you."

"Yes," said Dillard. "Aunt Flo helped take care of me growing up. She died when I was sixteen. In a car accident."

"She was a good-looking young woman."

"I guess so."

"She wasn't so much older than you. Seven, eight years. Did you ever think about her?"

"What are you getting at?"

"Well, maybe there's things you don't remember here as well. Auntie Flo—she had a temper? She was abusive, bossed you around."

"No."

"But on other hand, there was a kind of special relationship between you. Sometimes at night.. . . ."

A light came into Dillard's eyes. He realized where Wagoner was headed.

I thought of my own childhood, once upon a time.

"No. Not Aunt Flo." He shook his head, emphatic. "Absolutely not Aunt Flo. I just can't say what I think you want me to say. I'd rather die."

"Well, I think that can be arranged."

Wagoner's tactic was apparent. The attorney meant to build a case that Dillard's attack on his wife was rooted in revenge for years of abuse that had been suppressed. His relationship with Angela—the abuse alternating with sexual passion—had unleashed the anger, the rage, he felt for his dead aunt, and that had lay sleeping all these years. He had killed Angela, yes, but under severe duress, unconscious of his actions. This was evidenced in the way Dillard's mind had disassociated from the awful event, creating a fictional intruder.

"Not Aunt Flo," Dillard said again, but when he looked up I saw the weakness in his eyes.

I put a hand on his shoulder then, and our eyes met, and I reassured him the best I could, by looking into his eyes and smiling and giving his shoulder a gentle squeeze, the kind you give someone at a hospital, or a kid going off to war. I've reassured other prisoners the same way, guilty or innocent, sane or otherwise.

"I don't want to do my defense this way," he said, "I want a new lawyer."

Wagoner crossed his arms. He'd heard this kind of thing before; so had every attorney.

"Kaufman," said Dillard. "Jamie Kaufman."

Wagoner let out small laugh. A smile tempted my lips as well, not that I blamed Dillard. Kaufman was a hot ticket these days, ever since she'd taken a death row case out at San Quentin and gotten the man released. It was just that everyone else wanted her, too. Every accused murderer and three-time loser up and down the coast knew her name, and half of them had written her letters, pleading their case. The truth was Dillard had already drained his wife's estate to pay Wagoner's retainer, and Queen Jamie wasn't doing gratis work anymore. All her clients these days had plenty of money.

"I need some time alone with my client," said Haney. "I'll give you a call at your office, to talk strategy."

"Sure."

"Say hello to Elizabeth for me."

"Yes."

"She's a wonderful woman. You take care of her."

"I will."

I gave Dillard another pat on the shoulder. Then I drove home, taking the freeway down through San Rafael, winding under the high brown hills and the oak trees and all those houses with their glass windows, their redwood decks and their great big view of the world.

7.

Absent death, the attention flags. Every newspaper editor knows this, as does every writer of lurid tales.

Those of you who do not know my story—who missed it as it ran through the tabloids—may find yourself impatient.

Of what am I accused?

What are my crimes, you wonder, and what is my motive for this so-called confession?

To deceive.

This is what my enemies would say. To place the blame outside myself. To charm and seduce. And along the way take yet further pleasure in my deceptions.

As you have already seen, though, my charms are limited. There is a darkness in me I cannot easily conceal, and in the end such concealment is not my intention. I have my moments of compassion, of tenderness, but I do not mean to suggest this makes me an innocent, without ulterior motive. Even so my intention is to tell this story as straightforwardly as I can. Patiently, without rushing ahead. Because we learn from the telling, as they say, and there are pearls hidden in the meanest tale.

Still it's not easy. Like anyone, I want to be understood. I want sympathy. So I am tempted to jump ahead of myself.

To the evening of the Wilders' party, when I saw my wife from across the room, elegant and beautiful. Or to the instant later that evening when I ran from the arbor and pursued Sara across the soft grass. Or to the moment the next day when Milofski the homicide detective and Minor the prosecutor slid the photograph across the table and I closed my eyes, knowing what I was about to see.

I turned my head but my eyes were drawn back to that picture, just as my memory is drawn to it now.

To the figure splayed out on the bed. Strangled, in the way that Angela had been strangled. Other women, too, as it happens. I felt Detective Milofski's eyes boring into me.

But I am getting ahead of myself.

8.

Since the beginning of the Dillard trial, I had kept my distance from Sara Johnson. We met once quite by accident in the halls of the Civic Center, and this encounter ended up in one of the atriums of that odd modernist building, with its turrets and long, sloping halls. She wore a yellow shirt dress, belted at the waist.

"You've been avoiding me," she said.

"No," I said. "That's not true."

I was lying of course. One of those small lies that everyone tells, but I was trying to do the right thing. I wanted to drift out of her life without making a fuss. At some point, without really thinking about it, I had made this decision. Not quite consciously maybe, but I had made it. Even so, I dallied a moment there in the hall. Her eyes held a certain vulnerability, and a wildness, too.

"Are you feeling better?" she asked.

"More embarrassed than anything," I said. "What happened, that's not like me. It's not usual."

She touched me then and kissed me on the cheek. Despite my inclinations to the contrary, I might have responded more intimately, but we were in a public hall. The courts were down one end, the building department on the other, and there was a clerk walking by. As it was, I put my hands on Sara's waist and felt her body soft through the yellow dress.

"We need to talk," she said.

For some reason, I thought of Angela Mori. The victim has a role in the crime, too, some psychologists say. Or so I had read lately, studying for the Dillard case. Because every action is an interaction, and the criminal seeks a certain consent. Communicated through gestures. A turn of the head. An open door.

The clerk gave us a glance and I let my hands go from Sara's waist. It was for the best, I told myself—and I was grateful now for the passerby.

"I'm on my way to court," I said, though this wasn't quite true. In fact I was headed for the law library, in the upper reaches of the building, but admitting that would have given me excuse to dawdle.

"Call me," she said. "Come see me."

I kissed her then. I meant it as a quick good-bye, but I was sloppy and let the moment linger. The feel of her so close reminded me of that moment in her bed, back in her apartment.

I pulled myself away, avoiding her eyes, trying not to think of how she looked standing there in that yellow dress, leaning into herself, one foot tucked behind the other

In the end, though, I didn't go to see Sara. I didn't call. I concentrated on my work and tried to put her from my mind. I wanted things under control. The business with the ambulance had rattled me—and I did not want Elizabeth to find out about us. (Or that is what I told myself. There was an edge I walked, a line between revealing myself and staying hidden. It excited me, if I admit the truth; part of me wanted to be discovered.)

A few days later, Sara caught me on the phone. I was in my office going over my notes for the Dillard case.

"Jake?"

"Sara," I said. "I've been meaning to call."

There was an awkward pause. I could feel her wanting something more from me, there on the other end of the line. She was upset with me for not having come.

"Is it cold?" I asked.

It was the first line of a game I had played with her on the phone a couple of times. I resorted to it now, I guess, because I didn't want to face what was on her mind.

"Not now, Jake. I don't want to play that game. We need to talk."

"Is it breezy?"

"No, Jake. I told you. I don't want to play that right now."

"Oh. So it's hot. That's what you're telling me. It's hot. And I've just got on too many clothes."

Sara laughed, but it was a weary laugh, and I could feel things shifting between us. "Yeah, Jake. It's hot. But I don't know how much longer it's going to stay that way."

"You're wearing your summer dress?"

She didn't answer, and I felt the moment fade. My heart wasn't in it, and neither was hers. Maybe she was wearing her summer dress, maybe she wasn't. Ultimately that wasn't the point of the game. We guessed at each other's clothes, then took them off in our imaginations. The last time we'd talked like this, it had been a few weeks back, in the evening, while Elizabeth sat in her armchair in an adjoining room, reading one of her books.

"I can't do this anymore," Sara said. Her voice was earnest and sad.

"I can't either."

"The incident—the other day at our apartment," she said. "I know what was behind it, and so do you."

"You do?"

"The stress, the infidelity. It's too much. No matter how bold we think we are, how sophisticated. It's not healthy."

I didn't say anything.

"We have to make a decision. About us. Can you get away? Come talk to me."

"The Dillard case. It's got me swamped."

"Jake," she said. "I think it's gotten to a certain point. Either we do something with what's going on between us. Or we let it go. We end it."

Once again I was silent. In some ways I was surprised that she pushed things this hard.

"Deceit, it causes tension," she said. "It makes things build up inside. I pretend like I'm one way. Like I can do this kind of thing, but. . . . Why don't you come over, and we can talk."

"Sara . . . "

I heard sorrow in my voice, and regret, and for a second I didn't know what to say. I imagined Sara over me—that unfulfilled moment, when I had been reaching toward her—and though part of me wanted to go back to that moment, another part said no. Elizabeth was supposed to be home around five. She had gone off to another one of her academic conferences, but this one was nearby in Sonoma.

"It's not a good time," I said. "I've got this report. I've got to prepare my testimony."

"All right. If that's the way it is."

"I'm sorry."

"No, you don't have to be. I should tell you. Bill—he wants to get serious."

Bill was Sara's old boyfriend. A young attorney who lived in San Francisco's Mission District and did a lot of pro bono work for the Hispanic population there. They'd dated for several years and been on the verge of marriage before I stumbled along. My sense of it—she half wanted him, and half didn't. Her relationship with me was a fling, a way of escaping the decision. Flirting with the unknown. Underneath it all, she knew this as well as I.

"Not tonight," I said.

"Fine," she said, and hung up the phone.

An instant later it started to ring. I heard her voice on the answering machine. I was tempted to pick it up but it was the kind of thing, you're damned either way. In the end, I resisted. I gathered up my work and went home to see my wife.

When I got home Elizabeth had not arrived yet. I did not think much of it. She often dragged in late—distracted by a student or a colleague—and I figured she would be along soon. In the meantime, I went to my bookshelf and pulled out my copy of Kleindst. I plunged into my work with a renewed energy. Whether I did so as a means of escape—as a way of forgetting Sara—or in earnest pursuit of a greater end, I can't tell you. It may be that both things were true at the same time. Regardless, it had been a while since I'd read Kleindst, and I wanted to reacquaint myself with his ideas:

> *Situational memory loss is an acute form of amnesia, a blackout of memory that has its roots in early abuse, and typically reoccurs after an incident in which the suppressed abuse has exploded into rage. After such incidents, the afflicted patient will not remember his own rage, or the attendant violence, until much later, if at all.*

I thought about Dillard's story. The locked door, the intruder, the gamma hydroxybutrate in Angela's blood. I thought, too, about my moment with Sara, at her apartment.

> *If the memory does return, it is often fragmented, and marked by severe disassociation, in which the core identity of the afflicted individual separates from his or her actions— and as a result he sees the perpetrator of the crime not as himself but as a shadowy other. In such situations, the individual will go to great lengths to preserve this false view of events.*

It unnerved me, this analysis. I understood the tack Haney Wagoner wanted to take. Rather than fight the physical evidence, he meant to build his defense on the notion that the greater truth lay shrouded in his client's psyche, in a netherworld of abuse where memory had been destroyed and everything Dillard had told the police was not a conscious lie but a delusion, a metaphor for his unconscious state.

Would the jury believe this? More importantly, would they see it as reason for acquittal? I didn't know the answer, but I'd seen odder things happen in the courtroom.

A word of caution. This syndrome should not be confused with the feigned memory loss common among the criminal populations, and practiced with great flair by psychopaths and other malingerers.

I went on reading. About genuine amnesiacs and certified fakes. Case histories and interpretations. Rulings and counter rulings. Every once in a while I glanced at the clock. Nine thirty and Elizabeth still had not returned.

I thought about the case.

There was supposed to have been some kind of coordination between myself and Paulie and the other experts. A meeting of the minds, so to speak. So far it hadn't happened. It was Haney's job to bring us together, but he kept canceling, putting things off.

It was midnight before Elizabeth returned. She wore a peach-colored suit, well-tailored but simple, with buttons going up the skirt. And the necklace her father had given her.

"Where have you been?"

"At the conference. Didn't I tell you?"

I knew about the conference, as I have said. They held it every year. A psychiatric convention based on the healing power of myth. "Healing the Demons Within," it was called. Attended by teachers and shrinks and New Agers. This year, Elizabeth had been on a panel regarding the transformation stories: *Jekyll & Hyde, Frankenstein, Little Red Riding Hood.*

"Yes, you told me. I thought that was a daytime event. Over at five."

"That's true."

She lounged in front of her mirror unbuttoning her blouse. She regarded herself with a wry smile.

"Where were you then?"

"Out to dinner."

"With whom?"

"Fran."

There was something coy in her expression.

"I don't know if I believe you."

"You have your nerve," she said, then tossed her heels into the closet.

It was the kind of gesture she'd been making a lot these last few days, angry, with the source of the anger left unexpressed. Reflecting back, I realize I could have asked her what was on her mind, but I chose not to pursue the matter. Perhaps I already knew.

"Hard day?" I asked.

Elizabeth didn't answer, but continued undressing. She undressed with her back to me and soon stood naked except for the strand of pearls. I watched her put on her robe: raw silk, very fine and elaborately embroidered—a gift from myself to her a few years back, something we had picked out together in a shop in Chinatown. I would have gone to her then: lifting the robe from behind, sliding my hand around her waist, down into the open fold—but she bristled away down the hall. She poured herself a glass of cold Chardonnay and went outside to the deck. From behind the glass door I watched as my wife took off the robe and slid into the Jacuzzi. A green mist rose from the churning water.

I followed her out.

"We should go someplace together," I said. "Maybe to the coast."

Elizabeth's eyes were closed. She placed the glass of wine on the edge of the sauna now, her fingers still on the stem, and hung her head back, taking in the steam, letting her body go loose. Her neck was long and beautiful and she was wearing her father's pearls. The prison lights glistened on the other side of the inlet, and I imagined all those men inside their cells, unable to see anything like this.

I had done the right things in regard to Sara, I thought. I had made the right decision—though it occurred to me as I looked at my wife that perhaps the decision was not altogether mine. Everything could change.

"We could spend a few days," I said. "Maybe check out some property in Tomales. Just for fun."

Back when we first got together, Elizabeth had talked often about going over to Tomales, buying a little place close to the water. On the other side of the mountain, where things were quieter. It was a dream of hers, to escape to the coast—but she was not ready, not yet, to give up her work at the college.

I undressed and stood for a second naked outside the tub, feeling the night air. Then I dipped in.

"Just the two of us," I said. "We could spend some time together."

Elizabeth's eyes were still closed, her head back. My leg brushed against hers. I put my hand on her breast and kept it there and studied her open mouth, her turned cheek, and at the same time toyed with her father's necklace between my fingers. I tugged gently on the strand and imagined it breaking apart then, the pearls disappearing into the water.

"Please," she said. "Not now."

She took another sip of her wine, a delicate wine, fragile and well made, then climbed out of the sauna, trembling as she put on her robe.

9.

A few days later, I went to the courthouse to give my testimony in the Dillard Case. The Marin Civic Center was an unusual building, as I may have mentioned. A series of buildings really, interconnected, low and flat to the ground, trussed and arched in such a way so as to make it appear as if the buildings themselves were part of the hills. The walls were clay-colored, and the roofs were blue. A gilded tower, Hinduist in design but empty on the inside, without function, rose from a dome over the Hall of Justice.

It was early and the county workers were making their way up the terrace toward the building. A little dowdy, frumpy and out of shape, like county workers everywhere. I sauntered behind them, a bit envious maybe. At times I yearned to be one of the group, a regular guy, free of this wry smile, this hollowness inside. Meanwhile I could hear the thunder of the freeway in the arroyo nearby, and overhead a hawk was circling, feathering the currents above the road. I followed the workers up the hill and inside, near the elevator, I bumped into Minor Robinson. It wasn't surprising, I suppose; he was the prosecutor after all. We were dressed the same more or less. Blue suits and black wingtips. White shirts, ironed crisp. Such coincidences of wardrobe are not unusual among courtroom professionals but Minor and I bore other resemblances as well. I had been mistaken for him once or twice in these halls. Something about our build, maybe, or the way we stood.

There were other ways, too, in which we were similar. We'd both lived in LA for a little while. We'd both had ragged childhoods, and we'd both studied criminal psychology. Also we'd both lost our first wives, mine to drowning, his to cancer.

Now we stood together waiting for the Otis to make its way down. I was scheduled to testify, and Minor would cross-examine.

"So, are you going to take it easy when I'm on the stand?" I meant it as an off-hand remark, nothing serious, as I certainly didn't expect him to go easy—there was no reason he should—but I smiled anyway and we shook hands and he smiled, too.

"I'd like to, Jake," he said, "but the way you charm a jury, I can't take any chances."

We both laughed now. It was a collegial laugh: buddies, just joshing around. The truth was he'd bumped me from the county roster, and I knew he'd show no mercy once I was on the stand.

"You're on quite a hot streak yourself," I said. "It's been a while since you lost a case, hasn't it?"

"I lose my share."

"Don't be modest. With your trial record, you'll be in charge of the office before long. You'll advance."

"I'm just a county prosecutor. That's all I am. That's all I want to be."

"That's what I admire about you," I said, "your civic intention. It's pretty rare these days."

If he suspected I was flattering him unduly, such suspicion did not show in his face. He smiled gamely. His eyes were clear. Meanwhile the elevator took its time. A couple of trial lawyers drifted by, a man and a woman talking passionately not about law but about real estate, about the cost of property, about their soaring portfolios, they were sure, and a wine ripening in one of their cellars.

A professional romance, I gathered from their postures, the way they leaned toward one another. Illicit as can be.

They went on chatting as they drifted down that long hall, with its pink walls and open roof and palm fronds reaching toward the sun. The building was like a crevice in a mountain, a canyon that wound through the shadows then back into the open. There were spots of cold, of ferns and stone, and places where the sun poured down from the upper arcades. The couple wandered into one of those spaces now and high above I could see trumpet flowers tumbling over the terrace walls. I thought of the moment those two would spend together later, furtive, full of themselves, and I remembered my time with Sara.

"What do you get, a case like this?" he asked

I didn't quite follow. It seemed an odd question. "Money, you mean?"

"There's more to it than that, don't you think?"

The elevator was caught on another floor, and I regretted not having walked on, taking the stairs. Minor's shirt was very white, whiter than mine, and his collar starched, and I remembered someone telling me once upon a time that he'd studied to be a priest.

"No, people don't go into my profession for money," I said. "It's not something you get rich at. Not usually."

"No?" He was mocking me, I thought.

"The accused is entitled to a defense," I said. "And the law has long recognized that the circumstance under which a crime is committed, the how, the why, these are a legitimate part of the defense. A person's past, the abuse he has suffered, his mental state, his biochemistry—these are part of the circumstances a jury needs to understand. Not always, but sometimes, in some cases, such information is extremely pertinent."

Minor's face had gone hard but there was still that angelic look in his eyes, the soft voice. "You're good," he said, but there was something stern there, judgmental—as if he did not mean it as a compliment.

The elevator came at last and we stepped inside. "The schedule's been shuffled, you realize," said Minor. "You're not on till this afternoon."

"Yes," I said, though I did not realize this at all. I had expected to take the stand first thing.

"I guess you're Haney's lead psychiatric witness now that Madison Paulie dropped out."

"Excuse me?"

He smiled then: the same boyish smile I'd seen him give Elizabeth that night at the Blue Chêz—but there was something else there as well. Some pleasure at my expense. And I realized this was where he had been leading me all along.

"Paulie, and one of the others specialists, too."

"What do you mean?"

"Haney scratched them off the witness list. He's got Sherman and Lowe instead. They're scheduled for this morning."

My discomfort showed plainly, I'm afraid. My respected colleagues had bailed from the case and Haney had not told me. So I would be teamed with Sherman and Lowe, notorious experts of last resort, men who appeared routinely in every hopeless case between here and Eureka. The elevator door opened with an ugly jolt. As Minor and I stepped into the paneled lobby that led to the criminal courts our eyes met, regarding one another, and I studied those slanted eyebrows that someone had told me looked like my own, and the lips that were flush and wide and sensuous like a woman's, and eyes that were so clear and wholesome they surprised even me.

"I'll see you this afternoon. On the stand."

I nodded.

"It's all business, you know. I have the utmost respect for you as a professional."

"I feel the same."

"We'll have a drink after this is all over."

"Sure," I said. "We'll have five drinks. We'll have a dozen. Good friends like you and me."

"I look forward to it," he said, and there was that smile again, the eyes clear as a running stream, then he was gone down the hall. He was not the man he pretended, I told myself. He was looking forward to taking me on this afternoon. A skirmish, a battle—a little moment to relish—in which he would eviscerate me on the stand.

I wondered now about Haney's tactics in this case. It was more usual these days, at least in California, to fight the evidence during the first phase of the trial; then, if convicted, you came back with the psychological profiling to mitigate sentencing. Haney, though, had chosen to incorporate the psychological evidence into the main trial itself, as part of the argument against guilt.

The original plan had been for Paulie to testify on Dillard's general mental condition, then I would discuss Hayes Syndrome. But there had been no coordination between myself and the other specialists—and now I understood why. They'd never agreed to testify.

I ended up taking the stand in the afternoon, after Sherman and Lowe were done making fools of themselves and Minor had gutted them on cross-examination. The courtroom itself was a circular, windowless room with a dome roof and geometric shapes everywhere: paint-gilded ornaments embed-ded in the friezes, on the railings, even on the jury box. Haney Wagoner stood in front of me in his gray suit, with those round cheeks of his, those over-sized brows, and he didn't seem in the least conscious of the dilemma in which he had placed me. He took me through the usual preliminaries. Slowly, we made our way into the heart of things. I described the conversations I'd had with Dillard, and also the tests I'd administered to him: the Minnesota Multiphasic, the Rodgers Profile, the Kleinsdt Double-Blind.

Wagoner hitched a thumb into his waistband.

"Could you summarize your findings, please, as to the defendant's state of mind at the time the crime was committed?"

With Madison Paulie out of the picture, I had been put in an awkward position. My choices were not great. I could bend the evidence the way Wagoner wanted, or I could

leave him to twist in the wind. Neither one would do a lot to
enhance my professional reputation.

"Mr. Dillard is a borderline personality," I said.

This was a catch-all phrase, used differently by different
people in the profession, to describe behavior that skirted
the edges without falling into a clear category. Wagoner
hitched himself up. Underneath it all, he was a slow-witted
man. He regarded me with a kind of amiable wariness, still
expecting I meant to help him.

And all this time Minor watched from the prosecutor's
table, a man who missed nothing, sitting there with his legs
all askew, his pencil between his fingers, waiting his chance
at me.

"What do you mean borderline?" asked Haney.

"I mean the test results were mixed, and he was not easily
defined. He displayed some aspects of normalcy—but there
were also asocial tendencies. Whether these have their roots
in a native impulsivity, or a full blown psychopathy, or some
kind of childhood trauma. . . ."

At this point, the judge halted my testimony. He asked
me to start over: to elaborate my meaning in a way that
would not confuse the jury with psychoanalytic jargon.

"Could you define the phrase psychopath?" asked the
judge.

"I would be pleased to. Going to the Greek. Psyche has
to do with mind or soul. While pathology has to do with sickness. So a psychopath is one who suffers from an illness in
the soul, a sickness of the mind or spirit. In truth, in real life,
psychopaths can often be quite charming." I smiled at the
jury then. And several of the jurors smiled back. "They are
in touch with the basic manner of interacting with other
people. They emote quite well. They make good eye contact." I paused, my eyes skittering over the jurors, drawing
in first one, then another. I was flirting with them, I suppose, the way a speaker flirts with a crowd, bestowing a
glance here, there. "But their social dexterity is a mask.
Underneath, psychopaths lack compassion, as well as con-

science. That's the simplest way of putting it. Sooner or later they take off their masks," I made a gesture, like a man unpeeling a rubber face, "and they indulge their asocial impulses. Which in some cases, can be quite violent."

Wagoner looked distressed. I was engaging the jury, true, but the content of my remarks was not what he wanted. In the parlance of the law, psychopaths were not subject to much mercy. They possessed cognizance of their actions, that was the key. So in theory, if you wanted mercy from the court, you did better to show your client suffered from uncontrollable delusions.

Perhaps that was the intent of the next question. To address the matter directly, so that I could dismiss it—and remove the subject from the table.

"In your professional opinion, the tests you conducted, the interviews—did any of this suggest that Mr. Dillard was a psychopath in the sense of the word you have just described?"

I pondered a moment, feeling the jury watching, curious, desirous of guidance and insight. Wanting a show. (And I remembered then how Elizabeth, before we married, had come to see me testify, sitting in the spectator pew in her worsted suit, and how later when we'd kissed in the elevator it had been like there was some secret between us, some complicity in the crime, some voyeuristic pleasure, there in the Otis, touching each other all over.) Now my eyes met Dillard's, and I could see his misery and confusion and the jury saw me watching him and we all knew the trial had been going badly and his fate hung in the balance.

"I would say he displays tendencies in that direction," I said, "but I would not put him definitively in that category, no."

"Mr. Danser, didn't you indicate earlier in your testimony that there were contradictory indications on the tests you administered?"

At the prosecutor's table, Minor made a note. It was a

bad phrasing of the question. It gave Robinson an avenue to attack the results of my tests during the upcoming cross-examination.

"Yes, that's true," I said. "There are often contradictory indications on such tests."

"In your own conversations, with me, after interviewing my client, did you not suggest a quite specific clinical diagnosis, in regard to Mr. Dillard's mental state at the time of the crime?"

I realized where he was headed now, and what I was expected to do.

"No. I don't believe I made a definitive diagnosis, no"

Wagoner blanched. He didn't like the answer, but I was only telling the truth. He had talked, and I had listened, but I had never actually put forth the diagnosis he wanted me to repeat now, in front of the jury. I could not go out on that limb, not with Paulie gone from the case. I could not join the likes of Sherman and Lowe.

"You did evaluate my client for delusional thinking, though, and memory loss, did you not?"

"Yes."

Wagoner went to the defense table and gathered up his copy of Kleinsdt. He read from the text out loud, reciting the passage on situational memory loss. He pivoted on his heels and arched those eyebrows of his, trying to look confident, maybe, wise and capable. A man on the verge of bringing the truth to light.

"In your judgment, did Mr. Dillard suffer from this disorder?" he asked. "I mean, in the sense that he could have blacked out, and killed Ms. Mori in an act of unconscious rage that he would not remember later."

At the defense table Dillard was full of trepidation, I could see, and I felt my dilemma more acutely. This was the moment my testimony had been building to. I didn't want to punish Dillard for his lawyer's incompetence, but I couldn't manufacture the kind of evidence Haney wanted.

"I'd say it was possible, " I said, and I felt the energy leak out of the courtroom.

"Possible?"

"Yes. Possible."

"Possible," said Wagoner.

Wagoner repeated the word again, as if savoring it, as if he had won some major point. The truth was, my testimony was lukewarm at best, and he knew it. I had not given him what he wanted. He poked at me a while longer, the way one pokes at a piece of overcooked cod on a dinner plate, hoping it is really not so bad as it seems. Eventually he'd had enough.

"No more questions your honor."

Then came Minor Robinson. It would be anticlimactic now, I thought, his battle with me. For all practical purposes, I was a neutral witness. My guess, he'd sweet talk me, work out a gem or two for the prosecution, then let me go. But I was wrong. He went after me the same way he had gone after Sherman and Lowe. *Possible, you say?* With a glee that was a bit too personal. *What do you mean by possible?* Tearing me apart, mocking me. *So you have doubts about your own diagnosis, and changed it here on the stand?* Going on far longer than necessary, attacking me in a fashion I have no appetite now to repeat. I suffered. I squirmed. Later, I tried to shrug it off—a bad case, these kinds of things happen—but Dillard was doomed, and my testimony had done neither of us any good.

10.

The day the verdict came, it was windy out at the point. I was in my hot tub, out on the deck, trying to empty my head. To ease the stress, as they say. I had the radio on KPFA, the old underground station over in Berkeley. They were playing music from Windham Hill. Strains of Art Pepper mingled with ocean waves and the digitized crying of whales. The jockey mixed in a little Thelonius now and then, and mumbled something incoherent about the Coming of the One. On the other end of the cove, meanwhile, I could see a couple out on their deck, sunbathing. They lay leeward of Golden Hinde on the sheltered side of the bluff, and towering above them was Mt. Tamalpais, serene and dappled under the light, with its spiritual retreats, its spas, its Beaux Arts homes overlooking the canyons. From my deck, I could see the mountain, and Highway 101, too, rippling over the mudflats along the fringe of the old redwood forests that had been sluiced down a hundred years before. The sounds of the traffic carried across the inlet, and I thought about the people in their cars, in their houses, in the prison, all connected somehow in this current moment. Then the music was over. We were into the news hour, fresh atrocities everywhere. Serbs and Croats. The Israelis. A girl in Petaluma, kidnapped from her bedroom. And in Marin County, a verdict had been reached in the Dillard case.

Guilty.

Not just of murder, the jury decided, but murder premeditated—and rape.

Outside the wind grew erratic. It blew hard for a while, then died away. In one of its waning moments, I settled deeper into the water, closing my eyes, taking in the sun. Then the wind blew cold again, and I decided to hell with it. I got out. I put on my muscle shirt and my shorts and went down to the Paradise Gym. I worked out for a good hour. I made my mind empty, focusing on that depth, that place inside where there are no thoughts. It was hard to dwell for long on that inner void. The great wellspring, the Buddhists called it. I could sense its presence but I could not enter. Even so I kept pumping. I felt hot prickles on my legs. The sweat streamed down in rivulets.

I exhausted myself and went home.

By the time I returned to Golden Hinde, it was late afternoon and Elizabeth still hadn't returned. Though we'd made love several times these last weeks—rough and sensuous, a little bit frantic, my face pressed into her shoulders, her backside, my hands on her breasts—there was still something unsettled between us. I tried the hammock out front, despite the wind, trying to dream the breeze away, to drowse beneath the chill. For a minute I was back with my mother in Baltimore, and I was just a small kid with my head resting against her chest as she rocked on the porch. I felt my mother's hand in my lap. I squirmed at her touch. I raised my head.

Elizabeth came toward me now, walking up from the house. I was glad to see her. She wore a dark skirt and an imported blouse—a bright fabric, mottled blue and carmine. It was an exotic print, with buttons in the back. The color brought out the fairness in her skin. She approached me with a sense of purpose, a stride I recognized from the tennis courts.

I raised myself to the edge of the hammock and smiled. I wore a yellow polo shirt and white slacks. She faltered. My glance had an effect on her. My gray eyes, my good looks. (I have always had my conceits, my vanities. An infatuation with clothes and style, the surface of things. They overcome me even now, these frailties, a desire to look good, to be admired. Though perhaps these are not such awful flaws, I think. Perhaps they are common trade.)

"I want to talk with you," she said.

Elizabeth stood with her arms by her side, and her voice quavered. I heard her resolve though, and it occurred to me we were at a crossroads of sorts. "There are things we need to discuss."

"We lost the case," I said. "Dillard was convicted."

"I want to talk with you," she said again.

She folded her arms. Something in that gesture summarized everything that had happened between us in the last three years. There was the skirt that fell just at the knees; the hips slightly cocked, inviting; the lips upturned—but then the arms that protected the body, and the eyes, too, blue with skepticism.

She'd fallen for me three years ago because I was younger, because she liked my silk shirts and my tapered pants. She liked how I flattered her and touched her, roughing her up in ways other men were too polite to do. She liked our reckless courtship, and the idea that people talked, and the wild taste of me in her mouth as we tumbled about on those white sheets in her big house. She liked the vengeance on her husband—who'd not only been alcoholic and impotent but unfaithful in the bargain—and she liked, too, though she would never admit it, that her money gave her a measure of control.

"I've been thinking the same," I agreed. "We need to talk."

"Let's go inside. This wind, it carries a chill."

Her voice was impatient. In it, I could hear her Southern bearing. She could be sweet when she wanted, but at the moment she was full of bristle.

"Honey," I said. "Let's walk to the leeward side. Around the cove. We can talk as we go."

"Jake. . . ."

"Please—it's a nice day on the other side, out of this wind."

"If you insist."

We followed the trail winding along the bluff to the south. There were places along the bay where the path dipped to the shore—but these involved a steep descent through rocks and weeds. So we stuck to the higher spurs skirting along the cliff tops. The path went up, climbing inland through the scrub oak, then it snaked toward the water again, through a meadow of junca grass and poppies, emerging over an isolated cove.

The path widened. I tried to take her by the hand, but she shrugged me off.

"What's the matter?"

"You don't know?"

"Tell me."

"Your girlfriend. I know all about her."

I felt as if I'd swallowed something cold. The feeling moved through my chest into my stomach, then downwards, deeper into my core. Part of me had known, though. Part of me had guessed this was coming.

"I didn't believe it at first," she said. "Or I told myself I didn't. Then I realized it had been happening all along. I thought to myself, not again. Not this time. Why can't I have a life? Why can't I have what I want?"

She let loose then. Saying things that surprised me. You act the big shot, she said, but you don't make the money you pretend. You drain our account. My account. Business expenses. Trips to Los Angeles, Hawaii. And your office, why does it have to be so plush? The leather couch. The secretary. All of your suits, the car, the shoes. And the world's most expensive barber. All of it, for whom? Another woman. Endless other women.

"It's not true."

"You fucked Angela Mori, too, didn't you?"

"That's a horrible thing to say."

"Did you?"

That wasn't a question I intended to answer. The path climbed. There was no breeze and I could feel the sun and see the long drop down to the rocks in the cove. Elizabeth whirled on the path. She stood with her back to the water. Her hair was the color of mercury, of platinum under a white sky.

"I want a separation," she said.

I felt myself dividing, hovering, watching from the outside. I glanced at the rocks below.

Separation meant divorce. I had been through this before.

"No," I said. "Don't be this way."

I glanced into her eyes and remembered that moment between us in her convertible, the first time, before we'd kissed, when she'd been assessing me, trying to see who I was, knowing only the tennis court rumors, suspecting they were true, at least in part, but then studying my face, my lips, the watery glint in my eyes, the way I edged toward her—my hand already on her crepe blouse, touching the studded buttons—then she had pulled me towards her. She'd decided to take the chance. We'd revisited that moment more than once, I admit—it was a ritual: anger followed by passionate submission—but this time her eyes flashed and her lips curled. They were wet with gloss, those lips, and her eyes had been done with a faint blue. Something about her then—something in her face, maybe, in her stance—gave me pause.

Where had she been earlier this day? I wondered.

"Remember that night at Stinson Beach . . . "

"Stop it," she said. "I know how you are. I didn't know before but I know now."

Her voice was heavy with implication.

"Do you think I care about all this?" I waved my hand dramatically, taking in all of Marin. "The million dollar views, the houses, the swimming pools. Do you think I'm that shallow? Do you think that's why I'm here?"

Her lips trembled, and I recognized that trembling, and I thought for a minute she was vacillating.

"I'm sorry," I said, but she would not let me touch her. I had miscalculated. She had made her decision. It was all hers, I realized now, and she had made it weeks ago, perhaps months. Even so, I could see the hesitation in her eyes. She was still drawn to me, she still loved me. She was a sentimental woman, underneath it all, fragile, raw with disappointment. She needed to be touched.

There was still a future for us, I thought. I felt its inevitability.

"You don't mean this."

It was the wrong thing to say.

"I do mean it," she said.

"I'm a beast," I said. "I'm sorry." I tried once again to put my arm around her.

"Don't."

I was angry now, all of sudden.

"Fine," I said. "I'll go."

I went down the path. She didn't stop me. When I hit the bottom, I glanced back up the hill. There was a spot up there, under the oak, where you could look down at the house. She stood there now, I imagined, looking beyond me at the beautiful view, the blue water, the prison. Standing defiantly in her carmine blouse, in the high grass, fluttering like a flower in the wind. This way. That. Waiting for me to drive away.

I packed a couple of bags, then dragged them out to the car, laying my suits in the back seat so they would not wrinkle. I drove down to Sausalito, to Sara Johnson's apartment, not knowing if I meant to stop—but her car was gone. Off with her boyfriend, I figured. So I went into a diner nearby. I called Golden Hinde, thinking maybe Elizabeth would have calmed down by now and we could talk in earnest. No one answered. I sat in the café. I read the paper—a front page article about the Dillard trial, written by the court reporter. The piece was a hack job. The defense was one blunder after another, the writer said, and he took particular glee in my own blundering. There was even a picture of Minor tearing me apart on the stand.

I thought about going into the city, to one of the clubs. I could dance all night. I could lose my identity, become someone else. In the end, though, I didn't have the appetite. My last experience there had left me cold. So I drove down to Lucky Drive. I walked out to the edge of the marsh and stared at the prison, its lights reflecting off the black water.

I went into the trailer and took my box out of its drawer. I put it on the bed beside me. I didn't open the box though. I just lay there staring at the ceiling, at the darkness, listening to the wind.

PART THREE
Murder

II.

When I went out to my office on Monday, I found an invitation from the Wilders identical to the one they'd sent to Golden Hinde. I was on more than one list, I guessed, and they'd mailed it out to my work address as well. As my first appointment had canceled, I had plenty of time to regard it: the fiesta colors, the embossed lettering on handmade paper, all in a bright little envelope, the color of a gin fizz.

Barbara Wilder was an artist. It was a summer party, at the height of the season, so she'd lithographed an image of the sun into the margins—a sun with two faces sketched in the fashion of a Zen mandala, one side light, the other dark.

I wanted to go. The Wilder parties were giddy affairs, the evening was always beautiful, it seemed, and there was an effervescence in the air on that hillside up above Ross, a lingering sense of glamour, of wealth, of something about to happen. As I sat there alone in my office, the Wilder party suddenly seemed indicative of all I was about to lose if I lost Elizabeth. Those things did not mean so little to me as I'd tried to pretend the other day, out walking with Elizabeth, quarreling—when I'd waved my hand at the handsome world and said none of it meant a damned thing to me, not at all.

But I could go to the party without Elizabeth, I told myself. Though there was still a part of me, I confess, that hoped I could change things between us, back to the way they had been.

My office in those days was out in Greenbrae, in a suite on Sir Francis Drake Boulevard. An assortment of psychologists inhabited the building there. Sex therapists. Mid-life transition specialists. Gurus and transcendentalists. On occasion, our clientele overlapped. There were criminals among the enlightened, and vice versa, and they came to me at times with their violent thoughts, hoping to escape them, or at least find the deeper meaning therein. The truth was I could give them little solace, and I had troubles of my own.

If I were a Freudian, I might tell myself I was acting out a hatred with its roots in the womb. That I had never truly escaped my mother, so I was acting out the escape now as an adult, over and over, with the different women in my life. But Freud was out of fashion, so I had only my biochemistry to blame.

I glanced out the window and looked at the world. It was a beautiful day, with the cars glinting by and the sprinklers turning and an occasional blonde on the sidewalk. The magnolias were heavy with blossom and so were the jasmines and the azaleas and the bougainvilleas and the potato vines, too. The pears were in season and the apples and the cherry plums and they fell on the ground but were never eaten because there were just too many, the land was just too fruitful.

For me, though, things had been slow since the trial. People were canceling—even my pro bono clients. Maybe it was the summer doldrums, or maybe it had been my performance at the Dillard trial, but either way my two o'clock didn't show, and I sat contemplating that empty space between appointments. It grew wider, emptier. After a while, the phone rang. The voice on the other end was runtish and cruel.

"How are things?" Grazzioni asked.

I wasn't overjoyed to hear from him. My opinion, Grazzioni was a psychopath. A real switch artist, as they say in the profession. Someone who takes his own trip and lays it into your head, as if the ugliness comes from you, not him. When I'd interviewed him for San Bernardino County, I'd gone along with his game—all his crap and shine, the violent fantasies, the sex jokes—acting like it got my rocks hot, the way you feign such things on occasion (never mind it's not kosher for a psychologist to play such games, it happens sometimes, it's part of the routine), luring the patient along, finding out what you can. Later the bastard had tried to use it against me.

"When I saw you down at that club," he said, "with that girl, it made me remember old times. Our talks together. Then I see you on the news during the Mori trial. It gets me thinking."

"Listen, Tony, I'm kind of busy here."

"I heard you're remarried. New wife. She's from some wealthy family, isn't she?"

I'd spent enough time with Tony to guess where this was going. He had a gambling habit, and it got him in trouble. The murder charge had fallen apart but he'd done time for extortion, trying to get money to pay off his gambling debts.

"It's not going to work, Tony. So what, you saw me dancing in a club?"

"It's not the dancing, doc."

I should have gotten off the phone then, but that pig voice of his had a certain allure.

"You remember the man I was standing with that night I saw you, at the lounge there?"

"No," I lied.

"Well, he remembers you. Says he's made a number of transactions with you in the past. You had a different companion each time, he says. One of those companions was Angela Mori. He didn't know who she was at the time. Not until after the fact, he says, after she was dead. When her picture was all over the tube."

"He's pulling your leg, Tony."

"I tell you, I hear how she died, doc, I think about you, our little conversations. Well, certain lights go off in my head."

"Tony . . ."

"I think of those other girls. . . ."

"Tony . . ."

"You don't have to worry. My friend in the club, he's a dim bulb, low wattage. But me, I got needs."

"He's got me confused with someone else."

"That's a good one, doc. You and your ponytail. How many guys wearing those any more? Makes me think, deep down, you want to be caught. Sub-conscious, like. You know how I mean. Isn't that the way it is sometimes, guys like you?"

I fell silent. I was at a loss, I suppose, how to respond.

"I'm thinking twenty grand for starters. I wouldn't pinch you so hard except I got people breathing on me, too. You know how it is."

"I don't have time for this, Tony," I said at last. "I've got patients to deal with."

He started to laugh then. It was an ugly noise, that laugh of his. I hung up, but he had gotten to me. I tasted my heart up there in my throat. I glanced at the Wilders' invitation again and felt my old life slipping away, disappearing into that ugly laugh.

That evening, before the sun went down, I ran along the wetlands by the side of the bay, then underneath the freeway into Corte Madera. It was a popular trail, and once or twice I'd happened into Minor Robinson. He lived on the last street of a subdivision that backed into the old salt marsh.

I was brooding along with my head down, jogging on the berm above the swamp, thinking about the notion that the things that happen to us, they are not just arbitrary, but a reflection of our inner state. The turmoil of the self is the turmoil of the world. I did not really subscribe to such thinking, but there were times you couldn't help but wonder. As I ran, I happened to catch a glimpse of Minor's place below me, down a path overgrown with anise and salt grass: a modest house, small and tidy, built on a concrete slab back in the '50's. I had been inside once, at a retirement party for a colleague. (Elizabeth had been along, too, more quiet than usual, almost shy.) In the course of the evening, a couple of the guests had inadvertently locked themselves out of the house. They'd gotten back in easily enough, jiggling the slider around in its track. Even so, the episode had been a bit of a joke at the party and something to laugh about later, in the halls of the Civic Center: how easy it was to break into the Prosecuting Attorney's house. The incident really hadn't been so funny as people made out, but I remembered it as I glanced down into Minor's yard. The sliding door looked as flimsy as ever.

I kept running, jogging along.

I thought about Grazzioni and his threats. It is true, there are a few things I haven't mentioned here about Angela and myself. I pursued her for a little while, in the same manner I pursued Sara. She was reckless in similar ways, and I have a hard time resisting such women, but there is not really much more to tell. You can imagine our encounters: the dark rooms, our damp bodies, mouths wet with liquor. Unfortunately, Grazzioni could imagine it all, too. I feared he would tell Elizabeth, and other people as well, and let his imagination run. Even so, I had no intention of paying him. Because if I paid him once, he would only dial my number again. And he was a complication I did not need, no matter my karma, as they call it, no matter the illusory nature of the world and of the demons herein, self-created or otherwise.

12.

I was suspicious about Grazzioni, wondering why he'd shown up just now, if it was coincidence or if there was something else at work. In the past he'd tried to extort people for crimes he himself had committed—which is not uncommon with a certain type of criminal—and I wondered just how desperate he was, how short of money, and if he might be connected to Dillard and Angela in a way I was not aware of.

I decided to call Nate Jackson, a private detective who specialized in defendant work. He'd worked for Wagoner on the Dillard case, but I'd known him for a while—and he owed me a favor.

"Hey Jake," he said. "It's nice to hear from you."

Nate Jackson had a good phone voice, down-to-earth and sonorous. The detective was short on looks, though, obese and sweaty—and when you met him he gave off a rank odor from hauling around all that weight. Though I'd been face-to-face with him a number of times, it was still hard to put those looks together with the voice on the other end of the line.

"It's great to hear from you," he said again.

How I knew Jackson was on account of his daughter, Anabelle, who'd spent a few years up at Napa, in Ward C, in the wing for the criminally insane. Before that Anabelle had used to work as an au pair here in Marin. Then one of her charges, four years old, had drowned in a swimming pool under suspicious circumstances. Anabelle had been found unfit for trial. Meantime, as fate would have it, the state's case fell apart due to a mishap with the evidence. A few months later Napa let her loose. Part of it had to do with my testimony. I'd seen no sign of delusion when I re-examined her. Her reasoning was clear as a bell.

Her dad, Nate, was eternally grateful. The truth was I had just played it by the rules, but he felt like he owed me a favor.

"What can I do for you?" he asked.

"The Dillard case."

"I heard he was convicted."

"Yes." My voice cracked and I let it do so, deliberately maybe, because I wanted his help and his sympathy—and needed him to hear my disillusionment with the way the case had gone. Or maybe it was just the emotion of the last

few weeks. "Tell me, did you do an alternative suspect
search? Did Wagoner ask for one of those?"

He hesitated on the other end. Wondering why I was
pursuing this, I supposed. It was a good question. It could
be that I felt badly about Dillard's conviction. That I was
doing a little research, looking to help out on the appeal.
That may have been part of it—but if I am honest, I knew
there wasn't going to be an appeal. Not by Haney, anyway.
The money was exhausted, and Dillard would have to use a
court-appointed attorney now. No, I had another reason. I
wanted to know if Grazzioni could be linked to the case—
and if there was a way to get him out of my life.

"We did an investigation into the Dillard business, yeah,"
Jackson said now. "I had one of my people scope the police
records, looking for a similar MO, unsolved cases. He put
together a pretty theory, serial killer kind of thing. Wagoner
barely glanced at it. He was focused elsewhere, as you
know."

"Any primes?" I asked, and I knew I had to see that
report.

"There's a half-dozen strangulation artists out there. But
no one matched our scenario."

"How about Tony Grazzioni? Did you check him out?"

"Yeah—we checked Grazzioni out, but I don't know. My
feeling, the cops were off base on that murder charge down
south. They wanted him for other things, so they dragged
him in on that, too."

"That's his story. I don't know if I believe it."

"My opinion, Grazzioni, he's a peep show guy—so to
speak. Likes to look at funny pictures, talk to weirdos. Get
his rocks hot peeking at other people's laundry, then using it
against them. Extortion—that's his thing. That and gambling. Not murder."

"So what did Wagoner think of the report?"

"He didn't find much use for it, like I said. Except for
that motel story. He leaked that one to the press."

I remembered the story, unsubstantiated, but it had

made the papers anyway: a rumor that Angela had taken a room in a motel up in Novato, accompanied by an unidentified man. The only witness was a motel maid. "Guatemalan illegal, scared of her shadow," said Jackson. "*Vestido azul*. Blue suit, that's all I got out of her. Wagoner could have used her in the trial, maybe, to create reasonable doubt. To show there was another man, somewhere, that might have been the murderer. But no. He didn't think it was enough."

"I've got a job for you," I said. "Could you run a make on Grazzioni? Find out where he's living, where he's hanging around—that kind of thing?"

"All right, but I don't think you'll learn much. Not about the Dillard case anyway. He's got no connection to the deceased—if that's what you're looking for."

"Probably not." I shrugged. "But do you think I could take a look at the report you told me about? The one you put together for Wagoner?"

He hesitated once more. It was a confidential report, after all, and I could see the spot I was putting him in.

"Never mind," I said. "I'm sorry. I shouldn't have asked."

"No. It's okay. That case—it's still under your skin, isn't it?"

"I guess. But I know how these things are. In regard to client information. You can't just. . . ."

"It's okay. I can the get report for you. I have to dig it out, that's all. It's with my other files."

"I'd appreciate it."

"Meantime, let me see what I can find out about Grazzioni. I'll give you a call in a couple of days. You can swing by—and I'll give you everything at once."

"Thanks."

"No problem."

"I'll cover your time on this."

"Don't worry about it. I owe you, remember."

"I'll make it up to you," I said. "Give my regards to Anabelle."

"All right."

"How's she doing, anyway?"

"Great."

His voice weakened, though, the sound of a worried parent. His daughter was in Florida, the last I'd heard, working as a governess. Who had hired her, and how much they'd known about her past, those were other matters, and not necessarily a concern of mine.

13.

While Jackson tracked down Grazzioni, I turned my attention to other things in my life. Over the next few days, I drove out to Golden Hinde several times. I needed a few things at the house, it was true, but more than that I wanted to see Elizabeth. My timing was off—or her schedule had changed; she was never there when I arrived. I could have left a message, but I feared she would ignore it, or arrange for me to come out to the house when she was not there. I didn't want that to happen, so I risked coming to the house unannounced. I wanted to talk. I wanted to make it up between us. The Wilder party was coming up soon—just a week away—and I had it in mind that we might still be able to go together. Maybe I was foolish, the way people are foolish when they don't want to believe something is finished. Either way I drove out to Golden Hinde several times before at last I saw her car in the driveway—and I walked once again down the pink flagstones to our front porch. When she opened the door, she was wearing her reading glasses, new ones with tortoiseshell frames that gave her a studious look, big-eyed and prim.

"I just need to get a few things," I said. "I hope it's all right."

She dressed simply, in slacks and a white sweater, but her looks still affected me. She had on the pearls, of course, and studied me warily. Her eyes seemed bluer through the reading lenses, larger and more penetrating.

"I won't be long, I promise."

She was not quite able to turn away from me. Maybe she wanted to, I don't know, but something in her face softened and she let me in. I went into our bedroom and gathered some clothes I had left behind. Some good shoes, for the Wilders' party. My linen jacket. A silk tie. It didn't take long. I let the moment stretch, lingering in the closet there amongst her clothes. I touched one of her dresses, the sheer fabric, remembering her once upon a time as she leaned against the wall at some party, a little drunk, dallying, waiting for me to come to her, to take her outside and lean against her in the dark. I touched the collar now, I touched the hem. I let my fingers drift down the buttons.

On the dresser, there was a picture of her from when she was a child, maybe six years old, in a checkered pinafore with a wide collar. I picked up the picture and studied her eyes and they were the same eyes I knew so well, taking you apart in a glance.

At length, I left the closet. I found her at the kitchen table with books and papers spread all around.

"Research?"

She nodded, giving me the barest of glances then bowing her head to the papers. "You got what you came for, I assume."

"I'm glad to see you getting back to it."

"What?"

"Your book."

"I never really left off."

It wasn't exactly true. The last couple of years, after her father's death, she'd pretty much abandoned the project. On the table now lay the weather-beaten copies of some old folk tales, raw material for the analysis she'd started not long after her first divorce: a reinterpretation of the transformation stories from the point of view of depth psychology. *Bluebeard. The Bear's Son. The Handless Maiden.*

I knew her thesis. Stories like these were not just cautionary tales but talismans, messages from the nether land beneath human consciousness—and as such were vehicles for the re-integration of the self, the joining of the conscious and unconscious.

"What chapter you working on?"

"The last one."

"What's the title again, of the last chapter?"

Elizabeth was shy about this conversation, a little reluctant. Or maybe she just wanted me to leave her be. The truth was I already knew the answer. We'd had this conversation before.

"The Demon Lover," she said.

In her book, the last chapter and the first shared the same title. That was the way the Jungians were. Everything circled upon itself. When Elizabeth and I had gotten together, she'd been exploring the anarchic principle, and the importance of welcoming it into your life.

"How are they different," I asked now. "The first chapter and the last?"

Elizabeth pursed her lips, hesitating. She was a bright woman and understood my interest was not without ulterior motive. Even so, she couldn't resist talking about her work.

"The opening concerns itself with the act of seduction." Her eyes skittered over me. On the stove, a teapot had just begun to simmer.

"And the conclusion?"

"With fidelity. The union of the lovers forever."

Her face reddened. Elizabeth was a fair woman and reddened easily—sometimes for no reason at all, it seemed—but it was embarrassing her, this conversation. The teapot grew shrill. She pushed her hands against the table and stood up, brushing past me as she went.

I could ask her about the in-between chapters, I supposed, but I knew that answer as well. The middle chapters would be about the process of transformation: the movement from one state of consciousness to the other, and acceptance of the fact that each mode had within it the seeds of the other.

I watched her at the counter, steeping the tea in a china cup.

"Is there anything else?"

She stood with her back to me, in her white sweater and her slacks and her silver thongs.

"I just have a few things to get from my desk."

The truth was, though, there was nothing in my desk I wanted. I lingered in the hall, looking at pictures from our life together. Snapshots of our honeymoon in Bangkok. Our vacations in Cancun and Santa Barbara. The Mardi Gras in New Orleans. There were pictures of her family, too: her mother, her father, her maiden aunt. The pictures went back to when she was a child, and at the center of them all was a photo of her father taken some thirty years before. He stood in his polo shirt and his pleated khakis at some community event, a lean man who had the admiration of all concerned. Fair-minded and generous. Charming. With a debonair smile. The kind of guy who did everything well. Made all kinds of money. Played golf like a son-of-a-bitch. Killed a million Japs in the war.

Elizabeth came up the hallway now, her tea cup in one hand, a book in the other, and I knew her routine: how she would spend the evening in the bedroom, sitting and reading, propped up on her pillows—but before that there would be the sauna, out on the deck, and she would let the day soak out of her, her headed tilted back, eyes half-closed, not seeing the prison across the way or Mt. Tamalpais either, shadowing the water.

"You find what you came for?"

"Just looking at the pictures."

"Oh."

"Your father, he was a good looking man."

"People admired him. Yes."

"You can see his personality, here in the picture. You can really see the life in him."

My motivation was pretty transparent, I'm sure, but

Elizabeth seemed not to care. She was blind when it came to her father.

"He was a good man," she said. Tears welled in her eyes all of a sudden, and she choked up as she spoke. I knew the things that touched her, I admit, and took some pleasure in her reaction. I was manipulating her, maybe, but it is the kind of thing people do, sometimes, when they seek to get close to another. I'm not sure it is such a bad thing. "Did you find everything?" she asked. Though she was still angry with me, her voice was subdued and in her accent I could hear that small town where she was born. I could hear the railroad going by, and her Negro nanny, and her father, and the birds flocking to the pecan groves outside town, untended now, abandoned to the crows. I imagined for a moment the great swamp she'd walked in as a young girl, its fetid smell, the endless mud, and her laughter as the swamp stuck to her legs, sucking her deeper.

"I miss you," I said.

She raised her head, becoming larger for a moment, womanly and full. I saw her haughtiness through her tears, and in that haughtiness a pleasure that made me think things were not quite over between us. "If we let this separation go on," I said, "it might become permanent. You know how that kind of thing can happen. So I'm thinking, maybe we should get together and talk this out. Away from the house, on neutral ground."

I could not express it, but I knew what her father meant to her. Here in this living world—here in Marin, with the sky so blue, the clouds so white, the air so sweet—people like she and I, we consumed one another. We were hungry, the world was chocolate, it was candy. Her father existed outside time, a generous man who scattered his riches everywhere. Or so she believed. I had never had a father like that. I stepped toward Elizabeth now, wanting to possess her. To possess him, too, I suppose. She edged away. The Wilder party seemed infinitely far off, unimportant. I wanted her now.

"Why?" she blurted. The tears were back. They rolled vigorously down one side of her face, and her cheek twitched like that of a stroke victim. "The other women. Why?"

"My work . . ."

She laughed then, bitter.

"The stress . . ."

She laughed again. "Everyone has work," she said. "Everyone has stress."

"I know," I lowered my voice. "Come on. Let's be friends." I listened to myself, to the sweet murmur in my throat. She'd found it sweet once, anyway, and seductive, unable to resist the duality in my voice, the irony beneath the sweetness, the sense there was something on the horizon yet to come. "How about tomorrow, we go some place quiet. We talk. Maybe we go down to Tomales, look at some property. . . .

She stiffened now.

"I have other plans."

"Elizabeth . . ."

"No."

Her tone gave me no admittance. I should have dropped the matter there, but I couldn't help myself.

"Who are you going out with tomorrow?"

"That's really none of your business."

"You're still my wife. We're still married."

"We're separated."

There was silence between us. Outside I heard the sound of the insects in the grass and the birds, too, and the slow building of the tide.

"Fran," she said at last. "I'm going over to Fran's house. Girls' night out. Dinner and maybe the movies."

"All right."

I left then. I walked back up the flagstone to my car. I was alone, but the smell of her was still with me, and the imagined feel of her body. It was almost dark. I could hear the tide rolling in, noisy, pushing the brackish water up onto the rocks. It was a sweeping, primal noise. When I'd lived here it had used to catch me by surprise. Like something rising from within myself that I had forgotten. Then I drove away, back to my trailer on Lucky Drive.

On Saturday evening, I went by Fran's place. A jealous thing to do, but I couldn't help myself.

The house was lit up. Fran's Mercedes stood in the driveway, and there was no sign of Elizabeth.

She had lied to me.

Then I told myself no, that wasn't so—and I drove up Marsh Road toward Golden Hinde. Maybe Elizabeth and Fran weren't going out till later. Or maybe one of them had canceled. Or maybe Elizabeth had just decided to stay in, to be alone.

I won't bother her, I told myself. I just want to know. I just want to see her car in the driveway, at home.

The car would be there, I was all but positive. I was right. But there was another car in the driveway as well. A black Caprice.

I knew that car. It belonged to Minor Robinson.

14.

The next day I left my trailer and walked along the marsh. I had not slept much. I was feeling the way you might expect a man in my position to feel, clenching then unclenching, jealous, angry, then telling myself there was no reason to be so; all I'd seen was his car, after all. In my gut, I suspected otherwise. I was the fool, the cuckold. I walked onto the spit, to where the marsh meets the bay, where the dirt gets soft and the drainage rivulets intertwine. I began to feel morose—which is rare for me—and that moroseness turned to a feeling of nothingness—which is not so rare— and down there in the water, among the reeds, I saw a fallen log in the shape of a woman's body, I imagined, its arms still above water, and I stood on it for a while until those arms, too, submerged, then I stepped off. All that remained now of the log was a small, black hump above the water, and I knew that pretty soon the tide would come in and that, too, would be gone.

15.

I had a sensation those days that my life was building toward something. Toward what I didn't know. Though perhaps I am not altogether honest when I say that. I knew what had gotten me into this situation, and where it had led me in the past. Nonetheless, I felt at times an exhilaration—as if I were about to break free, to satisfy all my vagrant impulses—and then I would remember Grazzioni and his wild mouth, I would feel the trap closing in.

Around this time, I went over to see Nate Jackson, in his office in downtown San Rafael. San Rafael was getting spruced up—but it was always getting spruced up. There was an old mission at the center of town, and some high palms in front of the bank, but the large stores were vacant and the small ones were hawking used furniture and secondhand clothes. Jackson's place was over a busy corner on Lindaro, not far from the bus station. There was a lot of foot traffic here. Latinos from the Canal District. Day laborers, on their way up Prospect Hill. Winos stumbling in the lurid light—and locos, too, from the rehab centers that lay along Lincoln Avenue, housed in old bungalows, alongside all those motels and falling-down joints that lined the road out to the county jail.

Jackson's office was up some terra cotta steps in a deco building that had a fresh wash of paint but little else. I found him upstairs in a cramped office, sitting at his desk.

Nate was an unlikely detective. An obese man, like I said before, white-skinned, pale as a grub. He wore an open collar shirt, a couple sizes too small. He didn't fit too well in his chair either. He had a hard time getting around and didn't bother to stand up when you came in but instead shook your hand from behind his desk. The room had an unpleasant odor— acrid, ammoniac, like a house full of cats—and it was hard to hang around very long. Nate had that polished voice, though, soft and gentle. He had a reassuring manner, too—and also a network of moles and informants.

"Oh, my friend, I was just about to get in touch with you. We've been tracking your buddy, Grazzioni."

"Any luck?"

"He's got an address in the city—Polk Street. Only he hasn't been there for a while. Mail's piling up in the box."

"Yeah?"

"Yeah. So I had one of my operatives check out his other hangouts. Reno, Vegas—no one's seen him around lately. Word is, he's gone over his head with the gambling debts. Meanwhile he's been hitting his marks hard, all the people he can squeeze—but it isn't enough. He can't get the money."

"So he's in hiding?"

"Either that, or he's dead."

"Can you keep looking for me? I'll cover your time on this."

Nate raised his huge hand off the table, dismissing my need to pay. Then he glanced up at me sidewise, like one of those big animals in the zoo. His eyes were watery and sad. There was something on his mind. His daughter, I guessed. Though I didn't want to talk about her, I wanted to get that report—the alternate suspect search he'd done for Wagoner on the Dillard case.

"How's Anabelle doing?"

"Fine. You know how it is. You have kids, you worry about 'em all your life."

"She still in Florida?"

"Yeah, she needed some help recently. I had to fly down, get her resituated. You'd think, all the way across the country, you could escape the past, but no. Once something gets out on you, a certain rap, it has a way of following you around. Something happens—and it's your fault. Now there's talk of extradition. Of bringing her back here on the old charges."

"That's hell," I said.

I shook my head, and he shook his, and we both sat there for a while, thinking about his daughter Annabelle down in Florida. She was a big girl, like her dad. She had the same mannerisms, the same inflections. The same awful looks. Neither of them, I didn't think, would be invited to the Wilders' any time soon.

"The report?"

"Oh, yes."

He reached into his file drawer and handed it to me. It was quite a sheaf.

"I hope that helps you," he said.

"Thanks."

I held out my hand, reaching across the desk. He took it and didn't let go right away. His grip was moist, encasing.

"You know, remember, last time, on the phone, we talked about those records you have in your office."

"Records?"

"When you interviewed my daughter. You made a tape, took some notes."

He was sweating now and the smell in the room seemed to have gotten worse.

"Oh yes," I said.

"One of those sessions, remember, she said some things."

I'd interviewed her a few times. Early on, she'd been pretty disturbed and said some things that might be regarded as incriminating. Nate still worried that information might get out.

"Don't worry," I reassured him. "Those tapes are all confidential."

"This extradition talk. I'm worried they might subpoena for the information. The parents of the boy who drowned, they're influential. They won't let this thing go."

"The law protects us on this issue."

"Not always. So, well, I was wondering: how often you purge records?"

"I understand. If it makes you more comfortable, I'll send you the originals, and I'll clear the files."

"I'd appreciate that, doc. I don't know where I'd be without you. My daughter—she's a sweet kid."

"Very sweet."

In times of trouble, people find solace in the familiar. They seek out old friends, family. They find escape in routine, perhaps, or in work. Myself, I was no different. I was upset about Elizabeth—and I plunged into the report Jackson had given me. I studied it compulsively. It was the kind of work I'd done in the past—studying criminal histories, looking for patterns—and the truth was I found release in studying such documents, poring over the details. Such details could be gruesome but they hinted at something large and elusive, a deeper mystery I found difficult to resist.

I would skip the Wilders' party this weekend, I decided; there was no reason to subject myself to social scrutiny. Then I would change my mind. I vacillated, and in the meantime I studied Jackson's report.

There were two parts to the report, first the raw data — all the cases the investigator had pulled from the computer. Then his synthesis. I thumbed through the raw stuff first, hundreds of cases. Some were pretty famous. Dominique Dunne, the actress who had been strangled bare-hand by her husband, a chef at Wolfgang Puck's. Then Lolly Desanto, the politician's wife. And the socialite Marina Grabel. The list went on, young and old, known and unknown. A seven year old girl in a ditch, molested and asphyxiated. An old woman in a bathtub. Crimes by fathers and lovers. Mothers and friends. Brothers. Sisters. Drifting strangers.

The investigator had sifted though all these, looking for a pattern, for similarities with the Dillard case. In the end, it came to this. Fifteen women over twelve years, doped to the verge of unconsciousness, all strangled with a man's necktie.

You would think, somewhere along the line, someone else—a cop, a homicide detective, somebody—would have recognized this same pattern. But the cops were busy, and there were other factors, too, that muddied the waters. In ten of the fifteen cases, arrests had been made. Seven of those arrests had gone to trial. Five had led to conviction.

That was one reason, maybe, why no one had pursued the notion these murders might be related. A good percentage had been solved, or at least prosecuted. So there was no reason to suspect a common perpetrator.

There was another factor, too. The killer had altered his MO over the years. The drug had been chloral hydrate at first, then rohypnol, now gamma hydroxybutrate. In the earliest crimes there had been no sexual contact, but later there had been foreign saliva in the mouth, sperm on the clothes. In the latest incidents it appeared the man had molested the woman after she was dead. The killer was escalating. Less able to control himself, you might say. Or more bold, more brazen. Titillating himself—and the authorities—by becoming more intimate with his victims, and leaving more of himself behind as evidence. Or it could mean something else altogether. Maybe you didn't have one killer here, but several unrelated murders with similar MO's.

Either way, Nate Jackson had been right: there were no real links to Grazzioni. Or nothing I could use to scare him off me, anyway.

Ultimately the point of the report had not been to prove its case—but to give the defense a way to point the finger in another direction. To create a line of causality that led some-place other than Matthew Dillard.

I studied the victims.

Attractive, professional, women. Late twenties to early thirties. Seven from the Bay Area, including Angela.

Five more in Los Angeles.

One in Portland. Another in Vegas.

Then number fifteen, across the ocean, in Hawaii.

For each crime I recreated in my imagination the cir-cumstances of death. The time. The place. I looked at the pictures of the victim, and I felt, too, that odd, creeping, stalking joy the investigator feels. I have read about it in memoirs and psychological journals: how the investigator enters the mind of the criminal—and for a minute becomes the other, recognizing himself in the shadow he pursues.

Of the women in Los Angeles, two had lived in my old neighborhood, in the flats of Santa Monica. Another had worked in child services, in downtown Westwood, in a building not far from my office. The one who died in Vegas, I knew the hotel, the lobby, the slot machines. I'd taken business trips to Hawaii and Portland, too.

Atypical memory loss. Decompensation of the conscious mind. Blurring of dream and waking life.

As I have said, people who kill in a moment of rage, sometimes do not remember the act itself for several days, even months, years. It is as if the event took place behind a curtain, and the participants—the victim, the killer—are sil-houettes, shadows on a screen.

This kind of memory loss, though, is relatively rare. At least that is the current thinking. Most of these amnesiacs, in criminal cases, they are liars. In reality, they remember every instant. They relish their crimes. They compose mem-oirs, elaborate testimonials that feign innocence yet contain within them the secret admission of guilt. When cornered, they place the blame elsewhere—on some associate, per-haps, scheming against them.

But beneath it all, always, the nod and the wink. The charm. The psychopath's smile.

You, me, hey, we're all in this together.

16.

I'd always enjoyed myself at the Wilders' parties. They were well attended, rife with the sense of déjà vu, a sense anything could happen. This year, I hesitated. Elizabeth was likely to be there, and I had mixed feelings about seeing her in public. There would be a lot of other people we knew as well. Courthouse types and socialites, lawyers and shrinks, a swirl of chatter and the passing scent of celebrity. The Wilder parties whirled with personalities—people you knew and people you didn't, all glimpsed through the gauze of alcohol and ephemeral conversation: a client you hadn't seen in five years, an office worker from down the hall, the ex-mayor, a comedian friend of the hostess who'd just bought an estate down the road, ha, ha, and was appearing on Letterman later this week.

Though I had my reservations about going, I needed to get out. I needed to mingle: for professional reasons, if not personal: So I put on my evening clothes—my linen jacket, my white slacks, a pastel shirt—and drove out Sir Francis Drake to the little hamlet of Ross.

I wore a tie, blue silk, imported from Italy, knotted loosely about my neck. I had my sunglasses on and my hair tied back, and the breeze felt good as I whipped along the edge of the valley. The road was a four lane with a yellow stripe down the center, and the air was awash with the flowery, lotus smell of Marin. The road narrowed going into Ross, tunneling under some wild oleander: giant hedges dangling pink blossoms, poisonous and bright. It was a quaint town, a commons at its center. There was a market, and some filigree shops filled with old women and Italian pottery, and a corner with a little bandstand set up, where a trio stood playing Sufi music to passersby. I roared past them all into the hills.

The Wilders lived above the town itself on a hillside in the Kent Woodlands. The Woodlands, like all of Ross, had been a hunting grounds once. Now the old oaks were gone, and palm trees grew in their place, in front yards landscaped with colored stone. Wild parrots squawked in the eucalyptus trees, and the lotus smell was thicker then ever.

In the circular drive, an attendant took my car. I strolled under the arbor toward the house. A knee-high Buddha—Prajnaparamita, the contemplator of nothingness—stood in the rocks by the front door.

Mrs. Wilder and her husband had made their money in undergarments. She was a small, stylish woman, mid-forties, who wore her hair cut short and feathered close to the skull. It was blonde hair, heavily bleached. At the moment she hovered by the door, as she often did during her parties.

"Jake," she said, "how good to see you!"

I heard a murmur from the little group behind her, a whisper, I thought: my name and Elizabeth's, too—a whisper like the sound of those wild parrots chuttering in the eucalyptus. Everyone knew everything. The gossip was out.

Barbara Wilder hooked me by my arm.

"Let me give you the tour," she said. "I have a new meditation alcove, I'd love for you to see."

When she was younger, Barbara had been a painter of abstract portraits—but her subject matter had changed. Religious figures mostly, swathed in a mystical light. Lakshmi, the five-headed goddess. Philotanus, the god at the borders of heaven and hell. Our Lady of the Glorious Ascension, rising forever into the blue-tinged clouds.

"Life is difficult, sometimes, isn't it," she said.

"Yes," I agreed, and I thought about her husband. He always lingered near the pool during the parties, working the Tiki bar. They had a perfect marriage, people said, though they hung out at opposite ends of the house at such occasions—and I could not recall seeing them together elsewhere.

"We have so much, but in other ways we have nothing at all." She put her hand to her chest. "I find myself in crisis, teetering."

She moved closer as she spoke. She had a certain manner with visitors. We were her possessions in some ways, however temporary, and we needed to be cared for, arranged and sorted, placed in this room or that. Nonetheless she was a sincere woman and I understood what she was trying to tell me. It was an artful balance, this life of ours. Trapped between the physical and the metaphysical. Trying to come to terms with all you possessed (or wanted to possess). Hoping to transcend.

I glanced about for Elizabeth but she wasn't here, not yet, and it occurred to me that she might not come at all.

Barbara Wilder led me to the mediation alcove: a room in the center of the house, on a riser above the living room. The alcove had been an open pantry once, designed to service the dining room, but now it was empty except for a mirror and a gold-fringed pillow—and also a man with a wine glass.

"Oh, Madison," she said. "I see you're lingering here. It's a lovely space, isn't it."

"Very serene."

The man with the wine glass, it turned out, was Madison Paulie, the San Francisco psychologist who'd been scheduled to testify in the Dillard case: a thin question mark of a man, stoop-shouldered, with a wild mop of red hair. I had met him once before at a party in this same house.

"Pleased to see you again," I said.

"Likewise."

"I regret missing the opportunity to work with you."

"Me, too. I admire you hanging in there the way you did. That was a tough business."

"Thanks," I said, though I suspected he thought otherwise. It was a weak case, and I'd been made a fool.

Barbara Wilder had wandered off. I spotted her in the hallway talking to another guest. Another psychologist, I believed. Or maybe he was an interior designer. They were discussing the flow of her house according to the Oriental principles of Feng Shui.

"Very nice. The energy flows through the space and is yet contained. The Feng Shui, it is very good."

"Thank you. We've worked so hard to attain it. But I feel there is still something not quite right."

"Oh?"

"Sometimes looking at the garden, I feel askew. I'm ill at ease."

"Perhaps if you move the couch?"

Madison and I talked shop meanwhile, a little this, a little that. Dropping names, the way you do. He was very thin, as I have said, very long and tall, with unruly hair and a black mole on his cheek. He had an infectious smile but lugubrious eyes, a little sad, a little weary, like a man who'd been looking a long time for the solution to a certain puzzle but was beginning to suspect he would never find it.

Looking me up and down now all the while. Judging me, I thought. Though perhaps I was oversensitive.

"I saw you on television," I told Madison Paulie. "During the Rodriguez trial."

I meant it as a compliment, but his eyes narrowed.

"Disturbing case."

"Yes."

Rodriguez was the so-called Vampire Killer. During a long weekend at the height of his madness he'd mutilated a half-dozen women, hollowing them out from the inside. He'd eaten their livers, it was reported, drunk their bodily fluids, and in the end was captured at his mother's house on the front porch, blood on his face, and semen. His own semen, as it turned out.

"Clearly psychotic. Paranoid schizophrenic suffering

from auditory hallucinations. A candidate for the asylum if I've ever seen one. But the jury gave him death."

He shrugged, and so did I. It was one of the ironies of the system. The insanity statutes had been designed to provide treatment for those who suffered from verifiable mental illness. But such people were the ones jurors feared the most—and were least likely to send for treatment.

"On the other hand jurors love a sociopath," he said. "A guilty man who charms them with his talk, his smile. Who knows how to work the system."

"Those are the tough ones."

"Yes," he agreed. "I've been fooled myself."

Below us, more people had arrived. The meditation alcove was an unusual room. One side was open and gave you a sweeping view of the house. Two steps away, behind the partition, and you had the illusion of solitude. I took another drink. Paulie and I stood watching the crowd—he was a wide-eyed, curious man—then I saw Sara Johnson. I was taken aback, though perhaps I shouldn't have been; the Wilder affairs, they were those kinds of parties.

Sara lingered at the edge of the others, gangly, girlish in her white blouse and skirt.

Our eyes caught.

I was tempted to go to her—but then Barbara Wilder reappeared, Mike Milofski on her arm now, the homicide detective, a gruff man, perpetually unshaven. He was buddies with Minor Robinson and, like his friend, he was not very fond of me. The last time I'd seen him had been at the Blue Chêz, the day Minor came to our table. He'd been seated over by the window, with Minor and the rest of the Courthouse Gang.

Barbara Wilder had a camera in her hand.

"I'm getting pictures of all my guests," she said, "and I told myself, why not get you all together. Two criminal psychologists, and a homicide detective. A charming group, yes?"

"Ah, yes, Mr. Milofski," said Paulie, and it was clear immediately that they had met before, no introductions were needed. "My colleague and I here, Mr. Danser, we were just discussing our strange business. The strange bedfellows we make."

Milofski grinned at us. He grinned easily—a bearish grin that made you back up a step or two. "You shrinks and me," he said, "we're not quite in the same business, are we? But I guess I'll consent to a picture."

Barbara snapped the picture, then she was gone again—with her feathered hair, her luminous blouse, her earrings by Eisner. The place was filling up rapidly. People I recognized but whose names I could not quite remember. A anchorman from the local news. A congresswoman. A real estate broker whose face was on signs all over town—and who'd been to my office a few years back, plagued by dismemberment fantasies.

"From what you say, Lieutenant Milofski," said Madison Paulie. "I take it you have little regard for the psychiatric science."

"We cops, we clean up the bodies. We talk to the victim's relatives. We bring the criminal in. We have to touch him, feel up his ass, looking for weapons. It's not something the ordinary person has to suffer, putting your fingers up a psychopath's ass."

"Literally speaking, no," said Paulie, "but figuratively. . . ."

Milofski wasn't listening. He wouldn't have it. "No," he said. "To me, it doesn't make any difference if the guy's bipolar or paranoid or just a garden variety shithole. The crime's the same. The grief's the same. The punishment should be, too."

Paulie stood regarding the other man, his own eyebrows arched, neck bent in the manner of an inquisitive giraffe. "Then in your mind," he said, "there's no such thing as the person who suffers from irresistible impulse?"

"The impulse is in all of us," said Milofski. "The reasonable person, he tunes it out. He shuts it off. It's a matter of will."

"Free will," said Paulie. His voice was rueful, and I saw

the underlying exhaustion that comes to people in our profession. "Sometimes, no. It's chemical. There's quite simply something wrong with the brain."

"All the more reason to throw away the key," said Milofski.

I eased away. I'd been through this kind of conversation before and didn't want to go through it again right now. I worked my way to the other end of the house, through a marble verandah and onto the deck. Part of me was looking for Elizabeth, I admit, but she still hadn't come. There was a pool in the back, and a Tiki hut close by—a shed built for the occasion, covered with palm husks and well-stocked with liquor. Mr. Wilder stood behind the counter, in a pink polo shirt, pouring drinks.

"Gin," I told him.

"Certainly."

He may have had a perfect marriage, but I could hear the alcohol in his voice like an old friend and see something dreamy in his eyes. Prozac, maybe. Or Zoloft. The stuff of good relationships.

Through a window in the hut, I glimpsed Sara in her white dress. I lingered, watching her from behind. Mr. Wilder and a friend of his at the end of the bar started talking investment strategy. They were a bit drunk.

"Computers."

"No. Biotech. That's where you want your money."

"Same thing. It's all converging. Computerized muscle fiber. Bio-optics. There's some good companies."

"Opportunities, yes"

"This new drug, just around the corner. An investment opportunity if I've ever seen one. It'll let Baby Boomers live forever."

"Not all of them I hope."

"No, no. Just you and me."

There was laughter inside the Tiki hut. Meanwhile, outside, the torches were being lit and a jazz quartet was tuning up by the side of the pool. The water shimmered. Sara stood in the torchlight, handsome as I had ever seen her—but pretending she had not noticed me. I pretended the same and went back inside. I stared at my drink with the light-headed feeling you get at parties, hearing the vague chatter that veered from crime to real estate to the metaphysics of Waldorf education, and at the same time I sensed the blur of the world around me, of print skirts and sheer blouses, of silk suits and cotton polos, of hair just going gray, of black hosiery and flat bottom heels, the smell of cosmetics, of anxiety mixed with alcohol, of desire and giddiness, and the smell, too, of polyester damp with sweat. I finished my drink and sucked on the cubes and crushed the ice between my teeth.

A painting of Mt. Tam hung on the wall beside me. Another one of Barbara's I supposed, from an earlier period. An idealized view, a panorama of gentle slopes and lush gardens, of people at repose in hidden valleys. It was a shallow view of the world some might say—no menace, no danger— and suddenly I felt a rush of sympathy for them, all these people milling around me, and I felt pity, too, for Barbara and the rest, feelings undermined by that smile of mine, the smirk, tugging at my lips.

Milofksi elbowed up beside me out of nowhere. He and Paulie must have run their conversation dry, I figured, for Milofski to be sidling up to me. His demeanor was less than benign.

"Look what we have here."

The cop's voice was dark and ugly. I scanned the crowd. It took me an instant, but then I saw Minor Robinson in the foray below us, his gaze sweeping the room with that same steadiness it swept the courtroom. Behind him, a step away, stood Elizabeth. Her dress was flame blue. She lit up the place, and I felt a confusion in my chest.

Milofski grunted, a guttural noise like an elbow in the side, full of insinuating pleasure.

He knew the gossip, too. They all did.

Minor bent toward my wife, fondling her obsequiously, touching her elbow. He ran his fingers down her sleeve, bending to listen to a little something she had to say, a request; then he folded into the crowd, leaving Elizabeth alone in her blue dress. I took advantage of the opportunity and headed across the floor.

"Elizabeth," I said. My voice startled us both. It had a brute edge I had not intended, but the edge was there nonetheless. "What's going on?"

"I was invited to this party. So I came."

"You got yourself a date, I see."

"I didn't come with Minor." She held her features in profile, aloof. Her face had an otherworldly paleness and her lips were pink and her dress had buttons up the front, from the hem to the neckline. The buttons at the collar were undone, almost immodestly, so you could see her long neck, her breast line, and a hint of lace, too, on the camisole beneath.

"You walked in together."

"We ran into each other, in the parking lot."

She was lying, I thought. I could see the care with which she had prepared herself. Even so I felt the underlying pull between us. Her glance met mine, faltered. She reddened, breaking into an ungainly blush.

"Let's go outside."

"I don't think so."

"We can talk. Seize the moment."

"This isn't the place, or the time."

Across the room, I glimpsed Minor threading through the crowd, a drink in each hand. I took Elizabeth by the forearm.

"No."

I didn't listen. The room shimmered once again, and for a moment I was a man in a tunnel inside another tunnel, just emerging, squinting into the light. Elizabeth splayed her fingers against my chest.

"No!"

A hush rippled through the people nearby and I felt their eyes on me. I smiled, a wide smile, directed at no one in particular. My face burned. If I had left then, everything that followed that evening might have been avoided, but the entrance was knotted with people and Minor was almost upon us. So I went back the direction I had come, through the large French doors onto the terrace. Outside the jazz quartet had begun to play. The torchlight glistened on the pool. The Tiki hut had lost its artificial look and the band was playing a Chet Baker number, an instrumental that gave you the feeling as if you were floating on a glass ship over a blackening sea.

Sara.

She stood facing the bandstand, alone, all in white, a drink in her hand. A young man watched her from across the pool. In another moment, she would not be alone. The young man would saunter up to her, ask her to dance. I would lose everything.

"Dance?"

"What about your wife?"

"We're not together."

"I saw her."

"She's with someone else."

"So you'll settle for me?"

Sara gave me a smile, a wan turn of the lips that said she, too, wanted to tell me to go away—that she didn't like the way I'd treated her, ignoring her calls—but she wasn't quite able to say so, didn't quite mean it. Instead she placed one hand on my back, the other on my waist while I pressed her close, and we slid together across the dance floor. We did a couple numbers like this, Sara's cheek soft against mine.

"I have something to tell you." Her eyes were sad now, guilty looking, and this new sadness confused me.

"Now?"

"Yes."

We stopped dancing and went across the lawn toward an arbor near the garage. A white roadster stood slouched underneath the trellis, an old car, a convertible. I glanced back through the arbor to the lighted house and saw people moving inside, dancing, gliding about like figures in a dream. Then we leaned side by side against the convertible. It was a warm evening, and I took my tie off, draping it across the front fender.

"Things have changed for me, since the last time I talked to you."

"Things have changed for me, too."

"Bill, my boyfriend—he's in Santa Barbara. His father died."

"That's too bad."

"It was unexpected. Or he would have been here, too."

I didn't know what to say.

"We're getting married," Sara said.

"Congratulations."

She started to cry a little bit. I put my arms around her and she buried her head in the hollow of my shoulder. I patted her back, and at the same time felt her chest against mine, and then I started to kiss her in a manner that was not at all platonic—but rough and wanton, full of desire.

Sara responded at first. Then she pulled away.

"I can't hurt him," she said. "Not again. Not after what I put him through already. I told him we were finished once, and I can't do it again. There's this thing inside me, my heart, my soul, I don't know what you call it, but it's divided. Split in two. Part of me wants to be good, wholesome. The other part. . . ."

I kissed her again. I pushed her against the convertible.

"I shouldn't do this."

I slid my leg between hers, into the warm space between her thighs. One of my hands was under her blouse, the other up her dress. She wore white tights and I ran my hand up and down her legs, and her hips began to move despite herself.

"Oh, Jake. I don't know."

I had her down on the trunk now. She was splayed out like a star. I started to slide her tights down, and she held me fiercely. She was shaking. I ran a hand through her hair, trying to steady her. One of her earrings came off in my hand.

I put my lips over hers. I thought of Minor. I wanted to swallow her, to eat her whole. I thought of Elizabeth and the light in her eye. Sara pushed against me, thrashing now, panicky.

"Oh, Jake. No. I can't do this again."

I let her up. She ran across the lawn.

"Sara!"

I called after her but she kept going, a white figure disappearing into the blackness under the eucalyptus trees.

I followed, tucking my shirt as I went, putting myself together. As I crossed the lawn, I noticed two figures watching from the side patio. I wondered what kind of picture we might cut, Sara and I, and what these onlookers might think. I slowed down, walking now, and I realized who the two men were. Minor Robinson and Milofski the cop.

By the time I reached the front terrace, Sara stood talking to the attendant, asking for her car. I hung back. I did not want to make a scene. Once she had driven away, I came onto the terrace myself and asked the attendant to retrieve my car as well. Meanwhile Mrs. Wilder and some of the others loitered nearby, half-crocked. They made a noise like birds tittering, flying in circles around an abandoned nest.

"Leaving so soon?" she asked

"Work in the morning."

"On Sunday?"

"The Lord's work," I said.

This got laughs all around. Then the attendant appeared with my car and Lady Wilder indulged the prerogative of every drunken hostess, saying good-bye forever, touching me more than might otherwise be allowable, running her fingers down the front of my shirt. (For a second, maybe, I closed my eyes, feeling her fingers touch my chest, and in that instant I imagined myself driving down the streets,

"Where's your tie?" she asked, and I heard myself mutter something back, I don't know what, and she laughed, but I was not there, I was driving down the illuminated streets, and everything—the houses, the cars, the trees—they were all etched in a glowing, ethereal light, an aura—and I was headed deeper down those streets, deeper into myself.) Lady Wilder gave me a proper kiss then, sexless and gray, and I drove off. I headed for Sausalito, gliding over the same dark avenues I'd imagined just the moment before, illuminated now by the haze of the arc lamps overhead, by passing cars and the moon up there somewhere, glowing behind a cloud. I parked on a side street and walked up the back alley to Sara's kitchen. I knocked.

Sara opened the door, just a crack. The apartment was dark behind her.

"No, Jake."

"Would you like a drink?"

She hesitated. I could see the sadness in her eyes, the desire, and beneath them both a shadow, something she herself could not quite put a name to.

"Just one more time?" I asked.

Sara let me in, and I embraced her, and her body opened around me like a flower, there in the kitchen, and for a little while nothing else mattered anymore. I lost myself, there in the dark, and those moments, our last together, were as fierce and beautiful and pleasurable as any I have ever known.

Then the next day, in the early afternoon, the police came to me with the news that Sara was dead.

PART FOUR

The Accused

17.

What is the nature of memory? Chemical impulses, stored in the brain, like images on tape. Or something else, the soul maybe, examining the essence of existence. In many ways, I suppose, this is the riddle of life. *Who am I?* Why are some events replayed so vividly in our imagination, while others disappear as if they never occurred? Psychologists used to believed every instant of our lives was stored in our consciousness, waiting to be recalled. Nowadays there are different theories. We remember only in fragments, and fill in the gaps. So the self fashions its memories according to its current needs, and this process is ongoing.

Myself, I remember most vividly how I climbed over Sara in the dark, in her bedroom, and left her apartment as quietly as I was able. I had fallen asleep next to her on the bed, and I could still smell her on my body as I stepped outside. A car rolled by on a nearby street—I saw its headlights at the intersection, a sedan, there a minute, then gone—and I smoked a cigarette. I didn't smoke them often, but her boyfriend had left a pack behind. So I sat on the stoop, smoking, listening to the early morning sounds. I felt reconstituted, all the anger and confusion gone, everything back in place the way it should be, as if something had been set right inside me—all the parts aligned.

I got up to leave. I walked down the alley.

Did I hear footsteps then, an echo on the concrete, going up the way I'd just departed? Or was this something my imagination came up with later, a new detail, a brush stroke, an embellishment?

I awoke mid-morning, coming up out of the black heart of sleep with the same feeling of refreshment.

Things were going to be all right.

I went about my trailer and put things in order. I hung up my jacket, patting the pockets, and there I found Sara's earring, the one that had come loose in my hands the night before, out under the arbor. I placed it on the counter, then changed into my clothes for the new day.

I started to think about what I might do with my life.

I went to the gym. I did some chest presses, some leg pulls. Sit-ups and squats. I stared lazily around the room. A woman in gray spandex, dyed blonde, gazing ceilingward as she worked the treadmill. A brunette in blue, breasts taut beneath her polo shirt. A redhead on her way to the parking lot, to her Jag with the personalized plates.

For me, it would be time to hit the tennis courts soon. Maybe not here. Maui, I thought. Or the Virgin Islands. Or maybe I would go the other direction, deep into the heartland.

Studious shrink. Playboy. Man of contradictions—even I sometimes could not bridge the gap.

Back in my trailer I went through my box of keepsakes. Little things. Jewelry, photos. Remembrances of my first wife. Other women. Sara's earring lay still on the counter. It was over between us. The way we had made love last night, we were like people in the throes of a fever, but that fever had broken. She would not betray her fiancé again.

I dropped her earring into the box, fastened the lock, put it under my arm. I grabbed a clam shovel and headed out towards the bay.

As a psychologist, I know the importance of ritual. When we move from one season to the next, it is necessary to mark the changes. That's what I was doing then, walking through the high reeds along the Corte Madera marsh. I followed the path along an abandoned quay, where I could see San Quentin—with its grim, carnival towers, its stone walls and concertina wire.

I followed the spit out a little further, then went down the marsh bank to a high-water post. The water didn't come in this far anymore, not since they'd built the levee, and the ground here was dry. I dug a hole. My ritual. The box. Covered with dirt.

I was done with the past.

Elizabeth. . . .

I was not ready to let her go. I had put nothing of hers in the box. Even so, the box was under. I patted the dirt. There are some things we never let loose. The seagulls squawked. The pigeons squalled and scattered as I turned down the path.

As I approached the trailer, I saw a black Caprice parked in front. Minor Robinson leaned against the grill, arms akimbo, watching me approach, his jacket open to the wind. (I thought again of the night before, the car at the head of the alley, the footsteps.) He had come to talk to me about Elizabeth, I guessed, to duke it out, cowboy style, because he wanted her for his own. Then Milofski appeared in the doorway of my trailer, stepping out from within.

"What's up?"

Minor pointed at the shovel in my hand. "Where you been?"

"Clam digging."

"There aren't any clams out there."

"You're right about that. I couldn't find a single one."

"You're a funny guy," said Milofski.

"What's this about? What have you been doing in my trailer?"

Neither man answered. I heard something in the reeds, and a man emerged from the other side of the berm, a uniform cop, circling behind me now. His job was to chase me down if I ran into the tidal lands—but there was nowhere to go. Mt. Tamalpais loomed, the legendary maiden, half asleep, drowsing over the marsh. I saw the maiden's face then. The prominent cleft, up there in the ridge, her horse-teeth, her head tilted back, snoozing in the rock.

"Where did you go you last night?" Minor asked. "After you left the party."

"Elizabeth," I stammered, "did something happen to her?"

"This isn't about Elizabeth."

"Sara Johnson," said Milofski. "Your girlfriend. The one you chased across the lawn."

"What about her?"

"She's dead."

I glanced down. I felt the past and present coming together—and all the jagged aspects of my personality. I imagined myself underneath the ground, beneath that damp sand.

"That's illegal entry," I said to Milofski. "Unless you have a warrant."

"We just want to talk to you."

"I saw you in my trailer."

"No. I was only knocking. The door was open when we came up."

He was lying. The uniform cop was just a few yards behind me now, tightening the circle.

"What are you doing out of the office, Minor? You're a prosecutor, not a field cop."

"Lieutenant Milofski would like to get in pursuit while the scent's hot. You were one of the last people to see her alive. We thought maybe you could help."

I could imagine how I looked to them then: in my white shirt and my khakis, rocking back on my heels, eyes glistening with something like tears, maybe, and a small half-smile on my face. Milofski and Minor regarded me suspiciously, as if my posture proved my guilt.

"Do I have a choice?"

"You were with Sara, we know that. We saw you pursuing her across the lawn."

"I wasn't pursuing her."

"Be that as it may. Would you help us out with a statement?"

The three of us rode in Minor's Caprice, with the uniform following in a squad car behind. Minor told dispatch we were on the way. He was taking me to the tombs, to the jail beneath the Civic Center. When we got there, a television crew stood waiting on the sidewalk.

"What's this?"

"They must have got it off the scanner."

"What do you mean?"

"The murder—the press picked the news up, and they've been around all day. They're listening to the public frequency for every tidbit they can get. They must have heard you were coming."

"Christ."

"Sorry, I don't like this either. Except you know how it is once they get a bug up their ass."

I didn't believe a word. He could have picked me up without all the fuss, but he wanted to make sure he was in the footage.

The reporters came at us, and Minor went to speak to them. I turned my head and Milofski hustled me inside, down a long hall into the catacombs, to a dismal room not unlike that in which I had interviewed Matthew Dillard.

18.

They left me sitting in that room for quite a while, all alone. It was standard stuff no matter who you were. The cops wanted you to wait, helpless and bored. When they finally came, they came together. Minor still wore his suit coat. Milofski had taken off his jacket and stood brute-like in his wrinkled shirt sleeves. Minor sat across from me, but Milofski stayed on his feet, shambling around the table, a barrel-chested man, bearish and hungry.

Minor did the talking, at least at first.

"What we are trying to do here is get your statement," said Minor. "If you feel like you need a lawyer, you can get yourself one. I have no problem with that." His voice was flat and reasonable and in other circumstances I might have admired his professionalism, maybe, despite the enmity between us. "But I want to make it clear, you haven't been charged with anything."

Meanwhile Milofski paced behind me. The way he fluttered, just beyond my vision, got on my nerves.

"What went on between you two out at the arbor?" Minor asked.

Prosecutors don't often participate in the interrogation of a suspect, especially in the initial stages. Minor couldn't resist, and I knew why. He had always disliked me, and it gave him a special pleasure: the possibility he could prosecute me for murder and bang my wife at the same time.

"Sara and I had a relationship," I said.

He squared his shoulders and regarded me. He had an open face, and clear set eyes, and part of me could see why Elizabeth might be drawn to him. How she might turn away from me and all my ambiguities to someone who, on the surface of it anyway, played it all by the book. He was too calm, though, too self-assured—and I knew I should not trust him. Even so, I also knew there were certain facts that would cause me less trouble now, out in the open, then they would later on.

"The reason I'm hesitant to talk to you, I don't want that relationship dragged around in the paper," I said. "Things have been rough between Elizabeth and I. It's not going to make things any easier if my relationship with Sara gets dragged into the papers, alongside a murder investigation."

"I understand," said Minor.

"We both understand," said Milofski. "You don't want everyone to know you been messing around on your wife. But there's a dead woman here—and there's some questions we'd like you to answer."

Minor held up his hand, conciliatory. Playing the good cop now, keeping Milofski off my neck. Milofski would have none of it; he grunted in disgust.

"Sara came up to me at the party," I said. "She wanted to talk, so we went out under the arbor. Then we went our separate ways."

"What happened out there?"

I should cut this conversation short, I thought. I should get a lawyer. It's the thing you're supposed to do, everybody knows, but the truth is hardly anyone pays attention to that advice. The impulse to talk is strong. I wasn't any different from anyone else, but in my case there were other considerations. Sooner or later the cops would run a DNA test on the sperm, and they would figure out I'd been with her. Eventually I would need an explanation for what had happened between us, one that didn't put me out at her apartment. I decided to give it to them now.

"We were intimate."

"What does that mean?"

"For a little while, out at the arbor, we were intimate."

"You had sex out there at the arbor? Is that what you're saying?"

"Yes," I lied.

Milofsky burst in. "You are a quick operator, aren't you. You two, you couldn't have been out there ten minutes."

"I was trying to end the affair. It was all but over anyway, that's the truth of it. But she was an attractive woman, and we got carried away. We cared for each other, but Sara had a fiancé—and I told her she should get back together with him. That maybe it was over between my wife and I, but maybe it wasn't. I just couldn't give her a commitment. The situation was upsetting to us both."

"All this in ten minutes?"

"She ran away. Across the lawn. I followed her out there—but by the time I caught up, she had driven off."

"What did you do next?"

There were no witnesses to prove I'd been out to her apartment. No one had seen me.

"What did you do next?" Minor asked again. "After Sara left the party?"

"I had the valet bring me my car."

"Where did you go?"

"Home."

"To Golden Hinde. To your wife's house?"

"No. My wife and I are separated. But you know that, don't you? You've been out to Golden Hinde."

Minor didn't blink, I'll give him that. He wasn't about to admit what was going on between him and Elizabeth (or what I thought was going on, anyway), but people had seen them at the party. People would talk and the gossip would spread.

"I went to Lucky Drive," I said. "To my trailer."

"You know how Ms. Johnson died?" asked Minor.

"I only know what you told me."

"She was strangled. With a blue tie." Minor gestured at Milofsky. "Show him the picture. The one from the party."

Milofsky slid it across the table: a Polaroid taken the night before by Barbara Wilder in the meditation room. Madison Paulie stood on one side of me, Milofski on the other. I was smiling, standing there in my white coat—and my blue silk tie.

Minor took the Polaroid away and slid another photo across the table. A color glossy taken by the homicide photographer. Sara, prone on her bed. Legs spread. Milofski placed his index finger on her neck.

"Same tie."

"No."

"It's an expensive fabric. Not your usual."

"You're not listening." My voice trembled. The situation was coming home to me, I guess. "When I left the party I didn't have it on. I took it off up at the arbor. I must have left it there, draped over the car. The convertible. I remember quite distinctly."

"No," said Minor. "You didn't leave the tie behind. You had it with you. You had it in your pocket."

"How would you know?"

He didn't know, of course; he was just playing games, guessing. I glanced down at the table, at the picture of Sara. She was naked and her eyes had a milky look and her tongue was distended.

I sobbed.

"Why did you do it?" Milofski asked.

I put my head in my hands. I let it rest there for a long moment. I could feel the pair of them watching me, waiting for my answer, but I could say nothing. I was thinking of Elizabeth and Sara and all the women I had known over the years, and I was overcome.

I sobbed again.

Milofski repeated the question. His voice was gentler this time, a voice more gentle than I thought a man like him could have.

"Did she reject you?"

I knew what they were doing, how they were playing me. I glanced from one of them to the other.

"You offend me," I said.

"You killed her, we know that. "

"No."

"It's your tie."

"Why would I strangle her with my own tie?" I asked—and remembered Dillard saying the same thing. I was getting angry now. "Why would I do something like that?"

"I don't know. Why don't you tell us?"

"You can't keep me here."

Neither of them responded. Their eyes were cold as moonlight falling on a concrete stair.

"Did it ever occur to you, while you're here—playing this game, for personal reasons, trying to rattle me down—that the real killer is still out there? People are at risk."

They held that same composure, both of them, and I could see it didn't matter what I said, things were going to go a certain way. And it occurred to me that the DA's office would downplay the obvious similarities between Sara's murder and the Dillard case. At least for now. Because they didn't have the evidence tying them together. And Minor wouldn't want to risk the conviction he already had.

"You have to either charge me or let me go."

"We can hold you forty-eight hours," said Minor.

"I want to see a lawyer. "

Milofski swaggered up to me. His was face was inflamed and all the pretense was gone. "You're a goddamn liar."

"No . . ."

"We know what happened. You didn't have sex out at the arbor. No, Sara ran from you and you followed her home. You raped her in the apartment. You murdered her, and you think you can get away with it. That you can murder in cold blood and smile your way down the road because the rest of us are just too damn fucking stupid. Because you're clever and charming and it's all some kind of joke. I know exactly who you are. I know exactly."

He was in my face now, about as close as you could get without touching, hoping I would do something, anything, to give him an excuse—but it was an act, too. He knew where the line was, exactly how hard he could push. Minor watched from across the room.

"Call him off," I said to Minor. "I know my rights."

Milofski chewed his cud. He spat on the floor. Minor smiled. A tight smile, smug, angry—with the ends of his mouth turned up and his lips all prissed. I knew what that smile meant. He was going to take everything away if he could. He was going to ruin my life. Then the smile was gone and the pair of them left the room.

It took a while but eventually I got my chance at the phone. I called an attorney by the name of Ted Hejl—an old friend of Elizabeth's. He was an estate lawyer, not criminal, but he was an affable guy, and I needed someone to make the initial contact.

"You know more criminal lawyers than I do," he said. His voice held a certain reserve. He was from Texas, from a Slovak family in the central part of the state, turn of the century immigrants, but the old country had long since worn away. Hejl spoke in a gentleman's drawl that he could turn on and off at will. "I'm not sure I'm the man for this."

"Let me give you a short list," I said. "You call around.

Vouch for my character. And my ability to pay."

"I'll do what I can," he said. He did not seem as enthusiastic as I might have liked, but I gave him the list and he took down the names on the other end. I could hear him typing into his computer.

"Is there any one you'd prefer?"

I didn't hesitate.

"Kaufman," I said.

Jamie Kaufman was the attorney Dillard had mentioned the other day. Queen Jamie. Princess of the Damned, they called her. Defender of child molesters and incestuous fathers and women who'd murdered their own children. Bad company, maybe—but Jamie Kaufman won more often than she lost. She was busy, I knew, but she was good, and mine was the kind of case that might interest her these days. High profile—and the client had money.

"I'll call her," Hejl said at last. "And the others as well."

"One more favor," I asked. "Can you get in touch with Elizabeth for me?"

Hejl paused. When he did speak, there was the reserve again, the hesitancy. "I should tell you," he said. "I talked to Elizabeth a couple of days ago. She's considering a divorce."

I understood his hesitancy now; he was her attorney, after all, and maybe this was a conflict for him. I understood, maybe, but I didn't like it.

"Tell her I'd like to see her very much, if you could. Tell her, please. I'd appreciate that."

"I'll give her the message."

Our conversation ended and the guards took me down another hall through the electronic gates into one of pods, past a surveillance window, through the common area, into an empty cell. The walls were gray, and the energy inside the space was trapped. It was not a pleasant place. It had bad Feng Shui.

19.

In solitary, facing the possibility you may never emerge, it's funny the thoughts that come to you. You see yourself as a little kid. You see your mom across the room, with those big sad eyes of hers. You see yourself dancing through time, all the people you have been. Then you see your wife on the tennis courts on Magnolia Avenue, just before dusk, simmering along the blacktop in her white skirt, and you remember the perfect unity in that moment, all the desires of all your many selves focused on her shadow knifing through the twilight. You see yourself under the moon, sliding into the sauna, and you remember your hand rippling towards her. You put your lips over hers and feel her move beneath you, there in the water, your hand touching her breasts, her neck, the pearls, and then you hear the voices rising up through the ventilation ducts, *Who am I?*, the voices of all those prisoners, whispering in the darkness, and you fear you will never get out of here, that you will never attain the simple wonder you almost had, you almost possessed, that moment, sometime in your past.

Elizabeth did not come to visit me in jail the next day. Nor did Ted Hejl the attorney. Nor any of his emissaries.

Another night passed. Another morning.

Then a guard came and led me down the cellblock to a dank little room where the table and chairs were bolted to the floor and there was a panic button on the wall. I was told to sit and wait, and after about fifteen minutes a woman sauntered in.

She was a small woman. Not handsome, no, not by the usual standards, but there was something about her presence, very raw and blunt, difficult to ignore.

She took my hand.

"Kaufman," she said.

Milofski and Minor Robinson entered the room. A step behind them was a man in a white lab coat, carrying a black bag.

"Jamie Kaufman," I said. "I'm so happy to see you."

She smiled the smile of a person who understands her own importance. She was in her mid-forties, ugly and good-looking at the same time, well-endowed but slump-shouldered, with eyes that took you in at a glance and suggested she already knew more about you than you might like.

"Are you taking my case?"

"They don't have enough evidence to press charges. Not yet," she said. "So they're going to have to let you go."

"For the time being," said Minor. He was not pleased.

Queen Jamie had a glossy smile, not quite real, but underneath you could sense her intelligence, hard and wry. She had a dark complexion and mahogany hair. She wore a skirt suit, electric green, and a flame-colored scarf. She'd grown up in the garment district and moved to San Francisco a dozen years back. She'd made a reputation for herself on account of her unscrupulous behavior, and her ability to manipulate the press.

Minor's distaste for her was clear. "Before your client gets out of here, we need some tissue samples."

The man in the lab coat began to unpack his bag.

"A little taste of your blood, that's all," Milofski said to me. "Some hair. A scrape of skin."

I turned to Queen Jamie. "Do I have any choice?"

"They don't have a court order," she said. "But they can get one. My advice, give them what they want. Then let's be on our way."

The man in the lab coat clipped a little bit of my hair and put it into an evidence baggie. He scraped some skin from my fingertips. He drew my blood. I felt a horrible emptiness at the pit of my being. That emptiness grew larger as I watched the syringe fill.

"I'm dizzy."

Milofski laughed. "You're a gem, you know that. A price-less kind of guy."

He shoved a paper bag at me. The rest of them left, all but Queen Jamie.

I looked inside the bag.

My street clothes.

I grinned.

"I wouldn't celebrate yet," she said.

Her voice had a certain polish, but I could hear the urban squalor just underneath—the sound of a gull overhead, winging its way across the Jersey marsh. "Your friend, Minor Robinson, he's going to pursue an indictment. I'm all but certain."

"I'm innocent."

She gave me another smile now, all alone, one on one. It was the smile of someone who had dealt with a million cons.

When I got out of jail, there was nowhere for me to go. My trailer had been sealed off, and my car was in impound. Queen Jamie made arrangements; she found me tempo-rary quarters in an apartment owned by one of her cronies—a fellow lawyer who spent half the year down in Argentina. The building stood down by the old Corte Madera lagoon, on a road that twisted along the creek and ended on the backside of 101, in a wash of gravel and noise. From the street the place looked pretty battered, but inside a picture window overlooked the lagoon. It was sur-prisingly quiet. Through the window I could see an egret out on the water, and a path along the levee, winding back into a ragged bit of wetlands.

"I'd like you to stay close to the apartment," she told me. "Inside, preferably. Your face is all over the news right now, and I don't need the press camping outside."

"Will I have to go back?"

"Where?"

"To jail."

"If the tests go their way, if they have enough for an indictment. Bail's not likely, not in a case like this. They'll arrest you, and hold you for trial."

"I don't know if I can do that. If I can spend that time. My wife. . . ."

"Let's see what happens." She patted my shoulder then, the same way I had patted Dillard's. "Just stay put," she said. "I'll give you a call this evening. I have some ideas."

"My wife and I, we're estranged."

"I know."

"I'd like to see her."

"Your estrangement might be a problem, image-wise. Or it might be to our advantage."

"I'd like to see her," I said again.

"Just stay put, please. I'll call you later."

I hung close to the apartment for a while, but I needed air and the path through the marsh was too tempting. So I put on an old sweater I found in the closet and a fishing cap and some sunglasses and went out for a walk.

The path ran along a berm on the inland side of the Corte Madera marsh, then joined my old jogging path, snaking over this way from Lucky Drive. As I brooded along that trail, the terrain grew more familiar, and I remembered Minor Robinson's house nearby—on the last street of a subdivision that backed into the marsh. When I reached his place I glanced down and saw the sliding door still as it had been, crooked in its track. It would be easy enough to get inside, I thought; I could rummage through his life in the same way he and his buddies were rummaging through mine. It wouldn't be wise, though. Instead I wandered back through the marsh, thinking about Elizabeth. I whistled, but forlornly, like one of those loons that haunts the edges of the water.

Back in the apartment, I dialed Elizabeth's number. There was no answer. She had disconnected the machine. Dodging the press, maybe. Avoiding me.

Later that evening, Jamie Kaufman called, as she

promised she would. She was an abrupt woman, artless and disarming, but I was glad to hear from her nonetheless. She'd made arrangements for a strategy session in Bodega, an old fishing town up the coast, a couple of hours north. "Your wife will be there. And me, of course. We'll spend a couple of days."

"You talked to Elizabeth?"

"Not yet."

"I don't know if she'll go along."

"She has a role in this case—and she'll understand. It's in her interest."

"Shouldn't we talk in advance," I said. "Me and you. So you can get a clear idea. . . ."

"Friday—I'll be by your place. First thing in the morning. We can talk on the drive over. In the meantime, don't call her. Don't go to her. Let me handle this."

20.

I realized the police had no intention of letting my car out of impound, so I got myself a rental in Larkspur, a functional car, plain as they make them, that wouldn't draw any attention. Though my name and face were all over the local media, the man at the rental counter didn't recognize me. Or if he did recognize me, he didn't let on. Myself, I just wanted some breathing room. I drove out the Panoramic Highway up the spine of Mt. Tamalpais. It was a well-trafficked road, popular with tourists and weekenders from the city. For those who knew its history, it was a spiritual center, that mountain. The place where the old transcendentalists had meditated under the redwoods. Where Gertrude Stein had built a Buddha out of paper mâché, and the Dali Lama had rewritten the Tibetan Book of the Dead.

I knew the old legends, how the mountain itself was a

maiden girl, daughter of the sun, transformed to stone by her father when she got uppity and mean with greed. So now she lay slumbering, and her dreams manifested themselves in the lives of the people who strolled her hillsides. According to the stories our world would last only so long as she lay sleeping, dreaming, and would vanish when she woke.

I walked in solitude along the path towards the summit. Marin lay below me. Near the top, there was an outcrop known as Spirit Rock, and from there you could see in all directions, towards the Pacific, or east to the bay, or down slope to Cathedral Grove and Muir Woods. Closer by, I could see in a gully the remains of the Eighth Way Retreat, a commune that had been built on the shell mounds of the old Miwoks. I could see also the television towers across the narrows, on a hill in the city.

I stood on the outcrop. There was a smooth spot in the stone, worn by visitors, and I sat there and crossed my legs.

I closed my eyes.

The white noise rose from the valley floor, the sound of machines turning and people laughing and trucks grinding on the highway all mixed into one sound, I imagined, into the wind along with the noise of jackhammers and pneumatic drills. It was easy enough to imagine as well the whispering of the broadcast towers, the sales pitches and the news, all that noise in the wind. I concentrated on my breathing. Telling myself I was searching for nothing, just being, as you are supposed to tell yourself at such moments, though in reality you are searching for everything, this moment, up on the mountain.

For an instant, maybe, I felt the membrane between myself and the world dissolve.

I saw myself as if from above. I watched that man below me, with his legs crossed. He couldn't be still. He began to tremble, and in my mind's eye I saw him rise to his feet. He began to swear, to curse. To kick at the dirt. He pounded his head on the stones. He raged on—trapped in the maiden's dream—but the mountain was oblivious. The maiden went on sleeping until he exhausted himself, collapsing onto the dirt.

I had my moment of peace then.

I got up and drove down the hill. I was tempted to keep going, to drive and never come back. I could probably outsmart the police. I could probably vanish if I wanted, escape, change identities, never be found again. But there was no need for that, I told myself. I had a good attorney and my own wits. I would extricate myself, I was sure, though I thought, too, of what I'd told the police, how the killer was still out here, and I felt a sense of danger beneath the veneer of the moment, everything about to break loose.

21.

Just as she'd promised, Jamie came by early the next morning. She didn't talk much but took me straightaway to a barbershop out in Santa Venetia, on the north end of San Pedro. The salon, if you wanted to call it that, was on a busy intersection across the way from the Civic Center and the County Jail. There was a bail bondsman in the office overhead and a deli around the corner and attorneys of various stripes had hung their shingles on the side street that ran haphazardly up the hill, eventually narrowing to a bottle-strewn path that took you—if you followed it far enough—to a homeless encampment in an old creek bed. Men fresh out of jail took that path, sometimes—along with joggers who did not know any better, looking for a pleasant trail through the woods.

Jamie ushered me inside the barber's shop. Though it should have been apparent, I could not figure at first how come she had brought me here.

"Untie the pony," said Jamie.

"I don't understand."

"My man here, he gives the best cuts. And there's no appointments."

"I thought we were headed to Bodega." Lovingly, with a sense of impending loss, I touched my hair. It was superficial of me, I admit, but I can't help my concern with such things. Maybe it has to do with growing up poor, relatively speaking—and so appearance takes on an exaggerated importance. I notice the details, the cut of a man's clothes, or a woman's, their shoes, the car they drive, the style, the surface of things. Odd concerns for someone in my profession, perhaps, whose job is to look into the depths; but I would not be the first to insist upon a relationship, however skewed, between the surface and what lies beneath. "I have my own stylist," I said. "I get my hair trimmed every few weeks. This man here, he can tell you that, just looking. I don't need a cut."

The barber shrugged. He was a big man with a jailhouse tattoo. "If you're going to court, you need a cut," he said.

"Juries don't like ponytails," said Jamie. "Not on men. Or on women either, for that matter. And as far as the general public goes, you're already on trial. It's an image problem."

"She's right," said the barber.

"I look fine."

"Vain," she said. "Too conscious of style."

"No."

"Arrogant."

"That's not fair."

"You'll be convicted," said the barber.

In the end, I relented. I sat in the chair and the barber unbanded my pony, trimming it away, then trimming some more, taking my hair back shorter than I'd worn it in years. He did a reasonable job, I admit—and I enjoyed this new angle on my face, more exposed, more raw and wholesome. Nonetheless, when he was done, I looked down at the black and silver strands lying on my slacks with a genuine sadness.

"I feel naked."

Jamie ignored me.

"Your wife's riding down separately with one of my people. This'll give us a chance to talk, you and me, on the way over."

We headed north to Petaluma in her Mercedes, then took 116 slanting west toward the ocean. Jamie and I both sported disguises of a sort. Jamie wore her russet hair in a high swirl, with a curl trailing down each cheek. She wore brown slacks and red boots and except for her size did not much resemble the woman who'd picked me up at the jailhouse a few days before. My short hair gave me a regular guy look. I dressed pretty much the same as usual, a button down shirt, dark slacks, an Italian-cut Angora sweater. I wore one of those sports caps though, and dark shades, and for good measure a small mustache the barber had fixed on with adhesive.

"What do you need to know?" I asked.

We were on the outskirts of Petaluma now, working our way through mud hollows and gravel washes and high yellow hills that had been chicken ranches and dairy farms not too many years back. The old ranches had been divided into five acre lots, and there were mailboxes at the edge of the road, and gravel drives that snaked back from the mailboxes to hidden valleys covered with orange poppies. Mobile homes crouched here and there, and custom giants made of stucco and glass. Up ahead, the terrain changed quickly. It was apple country and the cider stands slouched along the highway.

"The night, at Sara Johnson's house, what happened?"

I told her the story then pretty much as I'd told it to the police. It had taken on the air of truth to me, as stories do when they are told often enough. I looked out the window. The apple country wouldn't last long. It was a transitional zone between estate parcels and the forest ahead, where the soil was full of rock.

"So you're telling me you had sex with this woman that night at the party?"

"Yes. Out at the arbor."

"You ejaculated?"

"Yes."

"While inside her vagina?"

"Yes."

"So those tissue samples out at the jail yesterday, when they come back from the federal lab, with the DNA analysis—the police are going to find a match. Your sperm, inside her vagina"

"I suspect so."

We drove through redwoods now, a forest of second growth trees, high and thin, shooting upwards from old stumps and pine needles and slanting creeks choked with debris. Overhead, above the crowning trees, I glimpsed the coastal light, the sky blue and dizzy. This was the other California, the one that was wet and damp, where the sun didn't quite reach the forest floor. Full of mold spores and ferns and ugly little plants that never stopped growing.

"What you just told me—it means we won't be in position to dispute the physical evidence."

"I understand."

"It's going to be your version—against theirs."

"Yes."

"Your wife seems somewhat confused. She's not sure what to believe."

"She knows I would never do such a thing."

"Did she visit you in jail?"

"No."

Another curve. Then another. After a while we crossed a bridge and pulled onto Highway One and started to climb, so pretty soon the road was high above the ocean. The blue sky had disappeared and it was all fog. I glanced at her hands on the shift knob. Nimble hands with red fingernails and a gold bracelet around the wrist. Plenty of jewelry. I looked her over then and she felt me looking and shifted gears in a way that told me I could look till kingdom come, it didn't matter to her.

"I asked Elizabeth some questions, in regard to some rumors I've been hearing."

"Elizabeth is a sensitive woman," I said. "She has a lot of pride."

"These rumors, they involve the prosecutor and your wife." Jamie downshifted, and I listened to the sound of the motor racketing against the hillside for a second, then fading as the cliff fell away. We thrummed along in the fog. Jamie shifted again and a thin smile creased her face. "I can understand how you would be reluctant to talk about it. Elizabeth certainly was. Except from a defense point of view, that kind of information . . . " She stopped herself then, and the smile faded. "Right now, a ceasing of hostilities might be nice. There's some things that need to be worked out."

"You're thinking about your fee?"

"Indirectly, I suppose, I'm always thinking of my fee. But before we talk about that, before the three of us have our meeting, I'd like you and Elizabeth to spend some time together. Talk things out, the two of you. You need a reconciliation of sorts. Nothing grand. Just enough so we can all sit down together and talk."

She drove firmly, in control of the road, and it wasn't long before we arrived. The lodge was just off the main highway—a wind-driven place on a bluff overlooking the ocean. There was no doorman, so I dragged our luggage into the lobby. The clerk was just getting to us when Elizabeth arrived. She wore those oversized glasses of hers and kept her hair under a scarf.

We didn't say much to each other in the lobby. It seemed like maybe we should have, but we didn't. I was an accused murderer, standing in the lobby of an oceanside bed-and-breakfast with my wife and my attorney, but there just wasn't anything to say. The clerk directed us to the second floor.

As it turned out Elizabeth's room and mine adjoined, and the door between us stood open. She and I lingered on either side of that threshold, regarding each other through the passageway.

"It's good to see you," I said.

"You, too," she said, though her voice was less than convincing.

"It looks like we got our trip to the coast after all."

"So it seems."

She turned her back on me, unpacking her things. "You can close the door if you want your privacy, " I said. "I won't be offended."

"I'm not frightened."

"No, of course not. There's no reason you should be."

The smell of the ocean filled the place. I put my suitcase on my bed. I went down the hall, exploring. There wasn't much to see, just the kind of trinkets and antiques you might expect in a place like this, driftwood and seashells and a few pieces of furniture from the old days, when this building had been the town grade school, or nursatorium, or whatever it said in the fine print on the tourist brochure. After a few minutes I came back.

The connecting door was closed.

22.

Later that day, at Jamie's insistence, Elizabeth and I descended the narrow sidewalk into town. Bodega Bay was a gray emptiness over the scudding ocean. It was wind and pampas grass and a jumble of houses on a ragged slope that tumbled down to the sheltered inlet below. We stood at the moorage and looked back up at the houses: the old clapboard ones and the fisherman's cottages and the smooth new homes of colored concrete and tinted glass.

"I'm sorry to put you through this," I said.

The road bent away from the moorage to the main street, more or less sheltered from the wind. Not much of a town really. A drug store and some tourist shops. We had done this kind of thing a hundred times during our marriage. Killing time, idling through shops. Elizabeth touched the merchandise and a kind of paleness filled my head. The world smelled of filigreed bedclothes and gray clouds.

We fell into this by rote, because we had done it before, and it was my best hope now, I knew, this roteness, the way habits of mind accompany certain actions, then the emotions follow, too, running down familiar paths, returning us to where we have been.

"I've done some foolish things."

"Indeed," she said. "You have."

We made our way down the street now to a cafe with clear glass windows and an asphalt parking lot. I got a glimpse of the two of us in the glass as we walked in. We were other people. A couple on holiday.

"But I'm not a murderer," I said. "You know that. I didn't kill anyone."

It is the kind of thing you are compelled to say in my situation but which sounds less believable with each repetition. As we sat there, waiting for our coffee, Elizabeth regarded me closely, in a way I had not felt her regard me before, and I could sense her mulling me over, reserving judgment.

Outside the window, the gray of the asphalt seemed to merge with the gray of the ocean. It was the endless gray of the coast, of rain in the distance and clouds overhead and salt-stained wood. Everywhere windows overlooked the sea.

"I still have my hopes," I said.

"About what?"

I smiled then, my best smile, sweet as I could, though there was a part of me watching as if from the outside, mocking. Even so, I was not insincere.

"I love the sound of your voice," I said. "You know, I always have."

In the past, when I said something like that, out of the blue, a compliment from nowhere, she would smile back, knowing my tactics but not caring, taking the flattery.

Even now, I thought, there was a hint of a smile. Even though she had all but abandoned me. Even though she had not visited me in jail.

"Hopes about what?" she asked

"Us."

The ocean swelled. A single black bird scuffled over the asphalt plaza; it perched on a stone, hunching there like an angry little man. Then it squawked and flew away, joining a dozen or so birds of identical carriage on a wire overhead. They were black-winged with gray breasts, and they surveyed the scene like judges on a panel, gazing about with hard black eyes.

"Don't push," she said.

"I don't mean to push. It's just—time is short."

"Once, I used to believe the things you told me." She had a little twist to her lips, a turn of the mouth that made her seem detached from what she said. "You're good at disguising things. Smoothing things over. A word here. A smile. Sometimes lately I don't know if I can stand to have you look at me again. Then, other times. . . ."

She let it trail off.

Some more birds had joined the others. They stood along the wires there.

"You shouldn't be seeing Minor Robinson," I said.

"He's an old friend."

"It doesn't look so good with him trying to put me away. Besides, it makes me jealous."

She didn't say anything to this. We finished our coffee, and the waitress brought the check and we went outside. The wind was loud and gave the sense of the world being reduced to its elements. The sidewalk was old and crumbling.

"I want things to be how they used to be," I said.

"You pursued me pretty hard," she said.

"I was head over heels."

She looked at me then with eyes that were very clear and I could see beneath her fragility an iciness that if you could crack it, if you could penetrate it . . . then. . . . I didn't know.

If you pierce our shells, crack the exterior, then. . . .

"I still the feel the same," I said.

She crossed her arms in front of her, clutching the wind-breaker close to her body. It was a practical piece of clothing, off the rack, plain and ordinary, not like her usual wardrobe at all. Her face was pale and young-seeming under the scarf. Here and there her hair tufted out, wispy and flaxen.

"Lately, I've been wondering if I really ever knew you," she said.

I took off the mustache. "I'm Jake Danser," I said, smiling like an idiot. "Your husband."

She didn't laugh.

"You and I—we got married too quickly. I did the same with my first husband. So I have to ask myself what was I drawn to. If there's part of me, just below the surface, that wants nothing more than to be humiliated. That seeks self-destruction."

"I understand," I said. "I have urges, feelings. I think things of which I am not altogether proud."

My face did something then. It went slack, I think. It became ugly and blank and I felt another part of me peering out. Elizabeth's eyes widened, and she backed away, and there was an instant then, perhaps, one of those extrasensory moments in which everything unexpressed between two people lies exposed, unfiltered. All that stuff hidden beneath knowing glances, unrecognized by the conscious mind, it was all there for a second, naked on the table. Just as quickly the instant passed. I smiled.

"I understand if you don't want anything to do with me. But I have one thing to say. I don't know if you will believe me—but it was over between Sara and I. That's the truth of it."

"You were with her at the party."

"No. Not until I saw you and Minor together. Then I wanted to make you jealous."

I remembered again that moment at Stinson, three years

back, with the gulls cawing and the waves crashing. There'd
been an instant then when things could have gone either
way. When she had looked at me, knowing who I was,
knowing down deep, but unable to resist. This was different.
She was fearful. I put my hand on her forearm. My grip was
loose, gentle. "We can change things," I said.

"No."

Overhead the birds burst from the wire. All of a sudden.
All at once. They cawed and griped their way across the sky.
Her eyes met mine again, and beneath the fear I saw her
confusion, her guilt. I saw in her eyes the admission maybe
that the trouble between us wasn't my fault alone. And I saw
desire, too. Then her eyes want vacant. She pulled away
from me and I followed her up the hill.

Later that night I stood by the side of my bed, undressing,
looking through the window toward the town below. I could
hear the sea. The adjoining door was closed, and Elizabeth
was on the other side. After our walk, we'd eaten dinner
together in the little restaurant next to the hotel. We hadn't
talked much, but she'd been gentler toward me, I thought,
and I told myself things were not over between us. After
dinner I'd taken her upstairs and kissed her on the cheek
and felt a small tremble shake through us both—but once
again she'd withdrawn.

There was still something between us unfulfilled.
Something waiting to happen.

Now I finished undressing and lay down on the bed. I
heard the ocean outside. I heard Elizabeth on the other side
of the adjoining door, settling in for the night. Then it was
quiet. The moonlight fell through the window, and the
clouds gathered and dispersed and then gathered again. I
thought of Elizabeth in bed, in her nightgown, listening to
the same roiling and crashing of the ocean, and I imagined
her face: her eyelids, her soft skin, her neck, her hair silver
as the moonlight.

Sometimes these kinds of things, these trials, they bring

people together.

I stood up.

I padded across the carpet. I listened. Nothing came from her room, no sound at all. I put my hand on the doorknob.

I held my breath. I wondered if she could hear me or perhaps see the shadows of my feet, blocking the light at the bottom of her door. I wondered if she lay there waiting for me, listening. Was she really afraid of me? Did she want me? I closed my eyes. I stared into that darkness inside of me. *I am innocent.* I turned the knob.

It was locked.

I went back to bed and lay listening to the sea, imagining the dark boats on the gleaming water, seeing them rock back and forth next to the pier, knocking one against the other, ropes dangling over the side, dipping into that sea. Then I followed, plunging into sleep.

23.

The next morning, we met for breakfast in Jamie's room. Her suite was more dramatic than either of ours, with a balcony overlooking the ocean. The breeze, though, carried too much of a chill to keep the doors open, and the glass was covered with gauze. Jamie sat in a winged chair with her legs tucked beneath her, casual, almost attractive in her oversized sweater, her black tights and white headband. Her features were sharp, her hair unruly. She was an amorphous woman, but underneath the surface there was something constant: something hard and glossy and insect-like.

Elizabeth sat on the other side of the table in a hardback chair. She wore a cotton blouse, open at the collar. The morning light was pale, without color—and she sat there in that stiff chair, vulnerable and a little bit wary, her lips turned in a wry expression I'd seen a hundred times. She had a touch of pink on her lips and her skin was luminous in the pale light.

"All of us have some decisions to make here," said Jamie. "Given the nature of the evidence the police have in their possession, this is going to be a hard case."

There was a natural antipathy between the two women. They'd met briefly the night before we'd driven down. Part of their conversation had had to do with Minor Robinson, or so Jamie had told me in the car.

"No one's pressed charges yet," said Elizabeth.

"They will."

"How can you be sure?"

"Well, there's the tie. They haven't proved it belongs to your husband yet, but. . . ."

"I left it behind," I interjected. "At the party."

"How did it end up at Sara's apartment, do you think?" Jamie crossed her legs. Uncrossed them. She leaned back and studied me through those black eyes, and I remembered the stories I'd heard about the way she grilled her own clients, deciding whether or not to take their case.

"I don't know, but I didn't have the tie on when I left. Barbara Wilder saw me. She can tell you."

"Regardless, we still have to contend with the sperm analysis—and the DNA report."

"I don't understand," said Elizabeth.

A smiled creased Jamie's lips. Her tongue darted out, and the smile vanished. "You better tell her."

"Tell me what?"

I glanced toward the window, struggling for the words. The sky through the gauze curtains seemed an infinite gray, vague and empty, and I couldn't find anything there to help me.

"The DNA," Jamie said at last. "When the tests come back, there's a good chance they'll get a match. Your husband's sperm, in Miss Johnson's vagina."

Elizabeth tilted backwards, lifting her chin, and I saw

confusion in her blue eyes.

"The arbor," said Jamie.

The confusion heightened, then disappeared, giving way to something else.

"Out at the arbor? You and Sara?"

I saw her disgust.

Whatever gains I had made the night before, I felt them slipping away. Meanwhile Jamie studied the pair of us, enjoying the moment: seeing me exposed, Elizabeth undone. Such voyeuristic pleasure—indulged at the client's expense, emotional or otherwise—was common enough in attorneys, I knew, though few would admit the fact.

"Let me explain what we're up against." Jamie directed herself at Elizabeth. "In a murder trial, to get a conviction, the prosecution has to prove the defendant had the opportunity to commit the crime, as well as the means, and motive." Jamie leaned forward, excited, and Elizabeth leaned away, growing paler in the pale light. Her blue eyes were as blue as I had ever seen them, and her features more delicate. "If the tie belonged to your husband, then it implies he had the means. And if the semen is his, it implies opportunity." Jamie was in many ways the opposite of my wife, with her harsh accent, her angular body, her crass, burnished looks. "Then there's the matter of motive. That's the other question the prosecution must address. Why would he kill her?" Turning to me, Jamie raised her eyebrows in mock bemusement. "There's a number of motives prosecutors look at in a case like this. We're going to see them all bandied about in the press. The prosecution will leak them out. You can count on it.

"The first thing they'll suggest is personal interest. Profit. What did you stand to gain from her death?"

I shifted in my seat.

"Nothing," I said. "How could I have anything to gain?"

"Maybe she was holding something over you. Threatening to tell your wife, ruin your marriage. They'll say that. Your wife has money. You killed to protect your stake."

"That's not true."

"The second is jealousy. Sara was leaving you. You didn't want to see her go—and you killed her in a fit of passion."

"No."

"And third," she said, staring at me dead-on. "Pleasure."

"What are you saying?"

"You killed her for the pleasure of it. Because you enjoyed the act itself. I guarantee—we'll see all of this, all over the papers. Unless Minor Robinson decides to drop this business."

Elizabeth shifted uneasily. Her wryness was gone and her self-assuredness, and I did not understand why. Her complexion reddened. It happened when she was embarrassed, or angry, or placed in a position that she felt unfair. She had Irish skin, and her face flared. I wondered why Jamie was doing this. She was trying to drive a wedge between Elizabeth and me, but I didn't understand why.

"But that isn't likely, is it Elizabeth? Your friend, Mr. Robinson, isn't likely to relent."

"I wouldn't know." Elizabeth crossed her legs and for a second I saw the Tulane girl in her, nose up, not so different than a photo in the album at Golden Hinde, in which she lounged self-consciously on the front porch of her Sophie Newcombe sorority some twenty-odd years before.

Jamie had brought up Minor deliberately, I realized. "Okay, let me tell you something," Jamie said. "This is going to be a taxing ordeal. Along the way, the details from your life are going to end up in the media. It's going to be draining emotionally and financially." Jamie smiled, and Elizabeth's color deepened. "I know you two have had some troubles lately. So what I need to know, Elizabeth. Are you willing to do this, or do you want to bail out?"

"What is it you want me to do?"

"For now: be the good wife. Or at least avoid consorting with the enemy."

Jamie kept on smiling. It was a soapy smile, unctuous, full of foam and froth. The kind of smile you could scrub the floor with, and the walls, and the toilet, and it would still be there when you were done, grinning up out of the washcloth. "Also, there's something else I want you to think about," she went on. Her eyes grew small and scarab-like. "It has financial consequences. If your husband is convicted, Sara's relatives will file a civil suit seeking financial restitution. They're going to go after every cent you've got."

"No," I said.

I stood up suddenly, and they both looked at me.

"No," I gestured fiercely, sluicing the air with my hand, a theatrical gesture, absurd and overblown, but I couldn't help myself. "I don't want my wife to lose her estate on account of me."

Jamie sighed, and Elizabeth glanced away, not believing me, thinking maybe I was in on this from the start.

"Elizabeth," I pleaded.

She would not look at me.

"There are two ways your wife could protect herself," said Jamie. "First, she could divorce you. That would protect her money in the event you are convicted. But, if she filed for divorce now, it would be ruinous to our case. As your lawyer, I would fight those proceedings tooth and nail. There are certain facts, certain indiscretions. I would bring them out. It would be very ugly, and very public."

Elizabeth reddened more fiercely—and it occurred to me what was underneath the surface between the two women. I should have realized it earlier perhaps. Jamie was goading her about Minor Robinson, threatening to make those rumors part of the case.

"The other alternative is to make some kind of agreement about the deposition of the money now. For Jake here to sign away his long term interest in your estate. Provided, of course, that you establish a defense fund right away."

Jamie's eyes shone with a hard glitter. She was securing her fee, I understood now, making sure the money would be set aside in advance. In turn, Elizabeth's estate would be protected should I be convicted. Elizabeth didn't say a thing. She cast her eyes to the floor, holding her silence.

"But you don't need to decide this now." Queen Jamie smiled. "Let's enjoy our breakfast."

The three of us left town together in Jamie's Mercedes, working our way back through the little communities along the Russian River—small towns that flooded every winter in the seasonal rains—towns full of gay yuppies and redneck hippies and meth freaks who hid out in slanted, decaying cabins built fifty years before by weekend anglers and escapees from the city. There was little talk in the car, just the pale hiss of the tires and the rush of the wind as Jamie wove along the black road through the redwoods.

Elizabeth's animosity was palpable, and more than a little of it was directed at me.

We put in at a gas station in Monte Rio. I no longer wore the mustache or the dark glasses, but the disguise did not seem to matter so much anymore. I got out to stretch my legs. The counter girl was young, maybe fifteen, dressed in a tie-dye shirt and leather sandals. She smiled in a quirky way, how girls at fifteen smile sometimes, aware of their sex, and she dropped her shoulder. I asked her where the mineral water might be, and she led me around to the cooler and I brushed up against her there by accident.

A red-headed woman in her mid-forties looked at me hard. She was the store owner, I gathered, the girl's mother—a spitting image only forty pounds heavier. She studied me, then raised a hand to her lips. Her mouth made a perfect oval.

"Aren't you that man—that psychologist I saw on the news. The one. . . . "

The pair of them looked at me in a kind of awe. I thought of the image of myself on the television since my arrest—playboy psychiatrist, psycho shrink—thousands of images broadcast over the air and duplicated so at any particular time there were hundreds of thousands of light-filled versions of myself in living rooms throughout the Bay Area. Mother and daughter seemed to glow, entering that space with me. The girl let her hand fall between her legs.

"Can I take your picture?" asked the mother.

Jamie stepped up. I thought she would forbid it, but she surprised me again. She positioned Elizabeth next to me and crowded herself into the frame as well. "I'm his lawyer, and this is his wife," she said. When the picture-taking was done, she handed the woman a yellow business card. On it was the name of an editor at one of the tabloids.

"Talk to this man," she said. "He might be interested in what you've got there."

Then sure enough, a few days later—after the defense fund had been established, and the documents signed—the photo appeared in the supermarkets. Below was this caption: *Amidst rumors that her client's wife has been having an affair with the prosecutor, legal eagle Jamie Kaufman swooped the accused and his wife off for a weekend of kisses and flowers while awaiting formal charges in the murder of Sara Johnson.*

Queen Jamie was ruthless. She'd gotten Elizabeth to set up the defense fund by threatening to reveal the rumors regarding Minor Robinson. Then, once she'd gotten the fund, she'd revealed them anyway. Whether they were true or not, it didn't matter. I understood her strategy. I would not be the only one to stand accused. Indeed, if Queen Jamie could help it, this trial wouldn't be about me at all. No. It would be about the prosecuting attorney—and his relationship with my wife.

PART FIVE

On the Run

24.

I was a free man, but the mechanism of the court can be a grinding thing. It holds you in limbo. Whatever my ambitions, I could not return to my life as it had been, and I could not start anew. The media was after my identity, chipping away. My practice had fallen to hell, and my trailer was under quarantine. Most of the time, I stayed close to the apartment—but I was anxious, fluttery, on the verge of flight. On one hand I could sense the police investigation moving inexorably forward, encircling me, but at the same time I could not escape the feeling that something unexpected was about to happen—some new revelation, some legal maneuver—to catapult things in a new direction. I exercised in the early morning, starting when it was still dark outside, running along the marsh, and as I ran I tried to put everything out of my mind. As the sky lightened I saw white egrets in the weeds and the houses pinkening along the marsh. The water was black. The tarn held my reflection and I saw myself moving on the water, running through the high grass under the telephone wires, darting by the pump houses as the morning broke and my shadow grew in the light.

The world shimmered.

I missed Elizabeth. I missed the age around her eyes, and the smell of her body in bed. I missed her clothes hanging in the closest.

I ran in the afternoons, too, and sometimes in the evening.

Elizabeth did not return my calls. The news stories angered her. I didn't like them much either. It hurt my pride to hear my wife linked to another man. I wondered how much truth was behind the stories, and I wondered if

Elizabeth realized the prosecution was manipulating the media as well.

Other times, I roamed in my car. Once I drove to Grazzioni's address, on Polk Street in the city, and found his mail slot overflowing. There was no sign of him. I visited the roadside motel where Angela Mori had been seen before she was killed. I settled into one of the chaises by the pool and unbuttoned my shirt and watched the maids in the outside hall, wondering which one had seen the man in the blue suit. I wanted to ask, but it was too risky; it would raise too much suspicion. Another time I went to Angela's old place in Mill Valley, a handsome little house with a picket fence and a birch tree out front, and I sat outside mulling her murder in my head, imagining the incident as Dillard had described it, and perhaps for a moment I felt a kindred excitement, erotic and cruel. I took a similar trip to Sara's apartment, and one furtive day I climbed the hill above Golden Hinde and watched Elizabeth below me, working in the garden. She was beautiful, all alone, digging in the dirt.

What did I mean to accomplish by these trips?

I could tell you I sought to vindicate myself in some way. That I was looking for some secret to be revealed. For some way of connecting events that would show my innocence. I could tell you this but there are people, I fear, who will never accept any explanation I put forth. I was doing what all criminals do, they say. Visiting the scene.

I had just come in from one of my jogs, one warm afternoon, sweating copiously as I came up the stairs. I heard the phone ringing and I approached it with the mix of dread and hope, knowing that it could be Jamie with news of the pretrial preparations—and it might not be good news. Instead, it was Nate Jackson. The detective's voice was so smooth and professional, so suave and out-of-the-blue, that it was hard to associate him with the overweight man who sweltered in the dusty office down off Lincoln Street.

"Tony Grazzioni's on the lam," he told me. "Some Vegas

people. He owes them money."

"Gambling?"

"What I hear, he's made contact with the DA's office, trying to work out a deal. One of those identity switches—if he gives them information on a case they're trying to bust."

"Where's Grazzioni now?"

"I'm still looking—and so are his buddies."

"So he's in hiding, seeking asylum. That's what you're telling me?"

"Yes," he said. "That's the way it looks."

I didn't like the news, but Nate's voice was soothing, and I was hesitant to let him off the phone.

"Anything else?"

"No," he said. "That's it."

"Call me when you find out more," I said.

"I will."

It wasn't the whole story, but at least I understood why Grazzioni had vanished. He was looking to save himself by turning state's evidence against his gambling buddies. I worried he might tell the police other things as well. Tony Grazzioni was clever, a shrewd talker. Adept at innuendo, shuffling the blame. If it were to his advantage to help Minor in my case, he might do that as well. He might do it just because he thought it was funny

The prosecution, meanwhile, was building its case against me. I read snippets in the paper, but there was nothing I could do. I hung close, like Jamie advised. I stuck to my routine.

25.

The next morning I went jogging through the marsh once again. It kept my spirits up to run along the berms, weaving through the cattails under the shadow of Mt. Tamalpais. I felt the power of the mountain as I jogged under its shadow.

I ran hard. I followed a chaotic, shifting path through the mudflats behind the tract houses. I ran past the high school, the drainage lagoon, the park. As I ran, the morning sun shone over the pond that lay behind the ranch homes on Lakeview Drive. The first cries of the children rose happily, shrilly, on the bike path as they scooted off to school.

When I came to Minor's house, I slowed to a walk.

There were parallels between our lives, it was true. We'd both been raised by single mothers. We'd both been on the fast track coming out of college. We'd both taken our first jobs in Los Angeles, and we'd both lost our wives and moved up to Marin.

We'd both studied human deviancy. His reaction had been to become a prosecutor. To drive the unwanted emotions underground. My own attitude was quite different. The nature of my profession was to understand, to enter into conversation.

I stood looking down at his house. On the walls of his office, at work, there would be charts, photos, clippings. An artificial matrix, a construction of his own making, of which I was at the center.

I thought about Minor and the resoluteness with which he pursued me. It wasn't right, no. There was something wrong in the clockwork. I glanced down the narrow path to the garden gate. I wondered if inside Minor's house—hidden in his papers, in his closets—I might find the key to the man, and I wondered if turning that key I might find my way out of the prosecution's trap before it was sprung. It would be a risky thing to do, though, foolish really. I kept on my way.

That afternoon I drove my rental back into Larkspur. There was a problem with the car—it was stalling out on me, dying all of a sudden—so I returned it to the rental lot behind the Exxon station there on the corner of Dougherty and Magnolia. Larkspur was a non sequitur of a town, hacked out of the redwoods some hundred years before. It had been a logging town once—full of speakeasies and strip joints—then the German dairymen had come with their cows, and the Italian farmers with their broccoli, and these were followed by vacationers from the city, building their cottages in the hills and the flats, coming every summer to picnic, to walk in the redwoods and hunt along the shores. Now Larkspur was a bedroom community for San Fran-cisco, and the streets were lined with foreign roadsters. The sun was out and the sky was blue. You could smell the money in the air mixed with the hydrangeas. Looming above were the coastal mountains, green as the rain forest, almost as lush. There were canary palms sprouting from the eucalyptus groves, alongside pines and oak and wild plum. It was a beautiful day, and in the air there was the sense of possibility. Eyes ran toward me and away and back again. For a little while, eating lunch, I felt as if my troubles would pass. I glanced into the eyes of an older woman, elegant, vulnerable. I felt a sense of well being just looking at her. Of recklessness and infinite possibility there beneath her tailored suit with the big buttons down the front.

Things will be all right, I told myself.

There were complications with my rental. The fuel pump needed replacing, and all the other cars were rented. They couldn't give me a new one till tomorrow. I walked home following the creek along the public trail, then back along the gravel berm to my place, overlooking the lagoon.

The afternoon paper lay waiting on the step.

The Johnson Murder
Dead Woman's Lover had Violent Past

Though Marin psychologist Jake Danser was released without charges in the murder of a county legal clerk, he remains at the center of the police investigation.

Research into Danser's background has uncovered a number of similar incidents, sources say, which suggest a pattern of violence.

Before moving to Marin, Danser was accused of

attempted rape and assault of a woman colleague he had met for drinks in a bar at Venice Beach. Though the charges were dropped, the incident was later cited in a divorce complaint filed by his wife at the time, Amanda Danser, who said her husband like to "troll for women." The complaint also alleged Danser had become violent in the couple's marital relations, and insistent upon anal sex.

Not long after the divorce, Amanda Danser died in a drowning accident off the coast of Baja.

In the Johnson case, the victim's boyfriend recently stepped forward, claiming the psychologist had attacked Ms. Johnson several weeks before her death, in an incident which necessitated the intervention of county medical personnel.

Sources within the DA's office have said that they are examining other leads, which may tie Danser to other cases—but the Prosecuting Attorney, Minor Robinson, would neither confirm nor deny these reports.

The story infuriated me. It was the kind of thing, once planted in the public mind, that would be difficult to dislodge. Not lies exactly but half truths, incidents exaggerated and made ugly by my first wife's lawyer in the heat of divorce—and now repeated without mitigation, without context. None of it would be relevant in court—but that wasn't Minor's goal. He had released this information to the press to help build a public case against me, to destroy my character.

That afternoon I got on the phone to Jamie Kaufman, because things were out of control, I thought, and I did not want my case tried in the media.

One of her assistants answered.

"I want this to stop," I said.

"Ms. Kaufman's in Sacramento. She'll call you back as soon as she's able."

"What?"

"She's in court. Another case. "

"I need to talk to Ms. Kaufman."

"I'll give her the message."

"Please."

Even if I had gotten through to her, I don't know how much good it would have done. The case was unfolding rapidly, and the reporters would not let it go. They pursued the bits and pieces of my life, and one of them managed to interview the paramedic who'd been called to Sara's apartment that day I'd blacked out in Sausalito. He was on the news that evening.

"Ms. Johnson had a bruised lip," the paramedic said. "There'd been some violence between them, that's how it looked—but she wouldn't admit it. Maybe she was afraid, I don't know. Either way she was covering for him, you know, how women do."

I flipped the channel. The stations had their legal analysts out.

I was guilty as hell, according to the expert on Channel 5. Innocent, according to Channel 7. A victim of city hall politics. A psychopath. A betrayed spouse. An unfaithful husband.

The late news added a new bit of information.

The investigators claimed to have found a vial of Liquid Ecstasy in my trailer: the same substance that had been in Sara's bloodstream the night she died.

That from an unidentified source.

My calm was gone. I paced. I called Kaufman again, but could not get through.

Finally, the next afternoon, she returned my call.

"We've got troubles," she said. "The DNA came in, and they got their match."

This shouldn't have been a surprise, but I felt the news like a blow in the chest.

"I just talked to Minor. I told him you would surrender without difficulty."

"Christ."

"He agreed to let me accompany you. If he gets down there first, he'll wait. He promised."

I thought of the footsteps I'd heard on the stoop in front of Sara's. Of the tie I'd left behind. Of the alleged drugs in my trailer.

"I'm being framed."

"Calm down."

"How can I calm down?" I shouted. "Minor's screwing me. And he's fucking my goddamn wife."

"I'll be there," she said. "Don't run."

I walked to the window and back. I thought of the rumors I'd heard about Minor and Angela. (That juicy bit of gossip, whispered in the Civic Center halls, linking them together. I hadn't believed it then, but she was a promiscuous woman, as I knew myself, forever walking the edge.) I thought about the way he'd torn me up on the stand. I went back to the window. I thought of his little house at the edge of the marsh. I thought about the way he pursued Elizabeth. Then I saw a pair of squad cars pull up outside, followed by Minor in his black Caprice. The cops came swaggering towards the front door. Minor brought up the rear, dressed in his blue suit. *Vestido azul.* The notion I had then, I guess it had been kicking around in my head for weeks, or even longer, but it seemed to come to me more clearly now, in a flash, as they say, one of those intuitive rushes that is like the first rush of a drug and doesn't seem quite real. *The man in the blue suit.* Then I slipped out the rear door, headed toward the marsh—and those high waving cattails—at a full out run.

26.

What I did next was impulsive and reckless. For this reason, some people will dismiss the suspicions I am about to cast as the kind of projections that guilty men make, trying to avoid responsibility for their actions. They will call me a liar. They will try to discredit my version of events.

For my part, I can only tell you what happened.

I ran, I admit. I can't deny that fact. I ran through the salt grass and the pickleweed. I didn't know if I was doing the right thing, or if it was utter foolishness, but I knew a rental car waited on reserve for me in Larkspur, and I knew the cops would be sending out a dragnet soon. I paused to catch my breath, wondering if I should go back now before I was caught running. I climbed the berm then to get my bearings. A row of houses lay in the hollow below me. Stucco cottages with wood shutters, all in a row.

And if I should go down the path now to Minor's house, I wondered, and be caught with my feet dangling from his window, what would I have to say then? How would I explain myself?

Minor fit the profile. A man in his late thirties, living alone, no stable relations. He'd had opportunity to commit those murders, and to blame others for his crimes. He worked in the prosecutor's office after all.

Murderers of a certain sort, they often collected mementos. Newspaper clippings, photos of the victims, even souvenirs from the crime scene. It was this kind of evidence I'd been after, I would say.

That was the kind of thing I could tell them if I were caught, I told myself, though I doubted it would bear much weight. The prosecution would cast some other motivation upon my actions, claim I was planting evidence, maybe, or just being perverse, the way certain killers are. (I do not deny there was an element of perversity involved in what I was about to do: entering another's man's house, rummaging through his things. But as to my true motives. . . .) For myself, the imperatives of the moment held sway. I went down the path and eased through the gate into Minor's backyard. I fiddled the glass door open and went inside.

I searched his office.

Rumor said he was the kind of guy who took his work

home, but I didn't see any evidence of that.

I opened his bedroom closet.

In front of me, on a closet pole, hung maybe a half-dozen dress ties. No-nonsense ties, solid colors, ugly as Jesus. I went on rummaging. On the top shelf, in an open shoebox, I found a revolver.

I searched the kitchen, then the living room.

Nothing.

In the nightstand, next to his bed, I found some refuse from his professional life, notes on stationery and pages torn from cop periodicals, old homicide reports and beneath these some bondage magazines. I opened one of the magazines and imagined Minor retreating here. Lying down with the centerfolds. Women in chains. Women bound and gagged. Women with cords around their necks.

It didn't fit his public image, these magazines—he would claim a professional interest, I was sure, a connection to some case—but there is always a fantasy underlife. A current beneath the current. A river that runs in the opposite direction, beneath the river we see. Even so, the magazines proved little, and I sat there wondering what to do next, thinking about the dragnet outside. All those cops looking for a man in a floppy fishing hat and a spandex jogging suit.

And what evidence had I found to save myself? I took off my hat, wiped my hands on my shirt, fumbled with my waistband, nervous like an idiot. I put my hat back on.

I pawed the drawer once more.

And in my hand: a small bottle.

A plastic bottle, about the size of a hotel sampler. Inside—a clear liquid. It drew my attention because I had seen little vials like this before, I could tell them. At parties. On dance floors. On the evidence table, in the courtroom, at Dillard's trial.

I opened the top and sniffed. No smell. I dipped in my finger. It tasted vaguely of salt.

Liquid X.

And if I showed my persecutors this vial, and told them I'd found it here among the magazines, what would they say? That I'd had the bottle with me the whole time. Hidden in the liner of my fishing hat, in the waistband of my jogging shorts. That I was planting false evidence.

"You brought the bottle with you inside the house, did you not?"

"No."

"What were you doing inside Minor's wardrobe—rummaging through his ties?"

I closed my eyes. There was a sound then, a small thump, like a rock splashing deep inside a well. A car door slamming.

Keys in the front lock.

I fell to my knees and slid underneath the bed. I heard footsteps shuffling down the hall, a man's footsteps. For a second I thought the sound was my imagination—I was over-excited, carried away—but then he was closer. I heard him sighing, urinating in the hall toilet. His footsteps came my direction, and I heard him pacing, closer yet, then he paused and spoke. Minor. On the phone, checking with the office. "Yes, one of the neighbors saw him leave his place . . . in his jogging suit, yes—and we're canvassing the neighborhood . . . I'm headed back to the office, but first I swung by my house for a moment. I had to grab something here."

He stood in the room not three feet away, so close I could reach out and touch his black wingtips from where I lay sprawled beneath the bed.

"My guess, the Queen told him I was on my way—and he ran." Minor laughed, full of some odd pleasure. "Yes, you're right. He's jeopardizing his case, this kind of behavior . . . Okay . . . Yes, yes . . . I'll let the field cops handle the search, and I'll be up to the Civic Center, twenty minutes."

I heard him shuffle through the nightstand, I thought—though I could not be sure— then I heard the drawer push shut. After a while he sat on the bed and the springs above me creaked with his weight.

He hummed. He tapped his toes.

He redialed the phone.

"Elizabeth," he said. "This is Minor."

I felt the anger inside me. "I don't want you to be alarmed," he said, "but Jake—we went to arrest him, and he's disappeared." I could picture Elizabeth on the other end: her porcelain skin and her blue eyes and her hair like a white flame. "I'll come out later this evening after the smoke clears," he said—and in the pause that ensued I could all but hear Elizabeth's Pontchartrain drawl, her voice soft and vulnerable in the telephone darkness. I'd lost her, I feared. She'd slipped away from me. "I'll stop by to check on you, to see if everything's okay. Meanwhile, keep your doors locked. I don't think Jake'll come out to your place, but he might."

His footsteps faded and I ventured out from under the bed.

I continued my search then, giving everything a second look—running my fingers over the ties, thinking about Minor at the same time, about him and Elizabeth out at Golden Hinde later tonight. Then I went back to the drawer in the nightstand and looked inside once again.

And beneath the magazines. . . .

"It was gone."

"What do you mean? You can't change your tune like this."

"I'm not changing my tune."

"You said the bottle was in the drawer."

"When I looked in the drawer a second time, it was gone. He had taken it with him."

"You expect us to believe Minor Robinson had a bottle of Liquid X in his nightstand, then took it with him. With what motivation?"

"Isn't it obvious? Can't you see?"

"You're a liar."

I went through the scenario in my head, imagining myself in that little room beneath the Civic Center, fending off their questions. I thought about calling Elizabeth now.

Warning her. Minor was coming to Golden Hinde this evening, after all—but she was no more likely to believe the story of the Liquid X than anyone else. The story was cock-eyed, I had to admit, and circumstances did not cast me in the best of lights. The only way to prove such a thing would be to catch the man in the act. I went to his wardrobe again. Minor and I, we resembled each other. If I left here later, after dark, wearing his clothes, no one would think twice. It was just Minor Robinson, going for a walk. If I could make it to the rental lot, I could get the car I had waiting. So I opened his closet. I took one of the ties and held it up to my neck in the mirror, just seeing how I might look.

27.

I've spent time with them, the killers. The psychopaths and the schemers. After a while you know how they think, the pure pleasure they derive from their actions. The ones who are honest, they tell you. If you let me out of this jail, they say, if you put me back on the streets, I'll do it again. There's nothing I enjoy better. Likewise you, they insist. You, too. I have gazed into their eyes, heard their talk. I have read the police reports and the psychological studies. I know how they operate. Polite as hell. Funny in an off-hand way. A self-deprecating charm. A series of encounters, the type any couple might have, a lunch date, a dance floor. Maybe you even have sex with the girl once or twice in the usual manner. Eventually, though, the moment comes. You hand her a drink, the girl gets sleepy. You view yourself from outside. The two of them. Him. Her. Watch as he removes his tie. She is thick-tongued, slurry. Gamma hydroxybutrate. Off to the land of no memory. The place of never was. He slips the tie around her neck. Her hands go up her throat, clawing. All the moments of her life rush into this one moment.

In the past, he used a prophylactic, but hell, he tells himself, I'll let myself go, and he imagines the evidence men examining the body—not just for sperm but for hair follicles, shreds of skin beneath her fingernails— and he wonders how long, how many times, before they make a match, before they find him, but they are fools, the trail is muddled, there are others to blame, easier targets—and anyway this is the thrill of it, now, when he parts her legs, kisses her lips, notices the skin already turning blue.

"What were you doing in his wardrobe?"

I wore his clothes now. I wore his jacket, his shirt, his tie looped around my neck. I had his revolver in my pocket. I knew his game, I could tell them. I knew who he was after next.

Elizabeth. My sweet wife.

28.

There was a part of me, foolish perhaps, that intended a certain ending. I would rescue my wife, and we would reconcile. Or there would be the hope of reconciliation, at least, if not love. Maybe that was the kind of ending I was hoping for as I retrieved the rental, then drove to Golden Hinde. Maybe it was as simple as that, though as a psychologist I know for every intention there is a counter-intention. For every expression of love there is an equal expression of hate. And for every secret revealed, another is more deeply hidden.

It was dark now, the fog came shuddering over the bay, filling the hollows—but I knew those roads pretty well. I eased up at a gravel drive across from our house. I didn't want anyone to see me, so I followed the gravel to the top of the knoll, then headed back down on foot. When I got close to the main road, I cut off and followed a culvert to where the creek trestled under the road. I scuttled down the dry bed toward the bay.

Our bedroom had a glass slider onto the deck. From where I stood, I could see Elizabeth sitting on the bed, raw-boned and beautiful, lost in one of her books.

I worked my way around to the other end of the house, to the French doors off the den. Soon I stood in the big room at the center of the house. The foyer was in front of me, opening to the bedroom hall. To the other side was the kitchen and the dining room table, and on the serving board near the table lay a set of cutlery.

A teapot whistled in the kitchen, low and faint at first, then louder. In a moment Elizabeth appeared, illuminated in the hall light, wearing her silk night jacket over her black pajamas. Her complexion was pale, as I have mentioned, and her hair was moon white, and she walked barefoot across the tile with her back arched and her head up. She was matter-of-fact in her elegance, and despite everything I found it hard not to reveal my presence to her. She glanced into the shadows, but she did not see me. The room was big, the shadows long and dark—and she passed through the vestibule into the kitchen to prepare her tea.

I listened to her clattering and tried to determine how I should position myself inside the house. Where should I be when Minor arrived, and what should I do? The impossibility of my situation seemed suddenly immense. I wondered if I should just step out of the shadows and tell Elizabeth my story. I imagined her backing away, not believing. It sounded wild even to me. So I stood in the dark. Then she appeared in the vestibule, holding a cup carefully in front of her, going back the way she had come.

I waited then, alone in the shadows, and what kind of thoughts went through my mind, what images, what impulses, I cannot tell you without you thinking the worse of me. I loosened my tie, though, I will tell you that much. I imagined Elizabeth beneath me in the dark, her body contorted in ways the body does not contort—no, it was Minor

she was beneath, not me (the faces shift, as in a dream)—
and then the pair of them jerked up, surprised, as I entered
the room from behind.

The doorbell rang.

Elizabeth answered and I glimpsed Minor under the
porch light. I saw his good looks, his boyish cunning. His
manner was reserved, like a good man back from some hard
duty. I watched his hand fall down her back and linger on
her waist, touching the robe, the soft fabric; then they kissed
and I felt something like a knife in my heart. I glanced at the
shelf then, at the little statue there, the lascivious Buddha
with his hands on his belly, laughing. Maybe this was the real
reason I had come. To watch. To discover for myself if the
rumors were true. Part of me was sickened and fearful, but
another part relished the moment. As Elizabeth turned
from him, I glimpsed her face. Her lips were gaping and
voluptuous, and her eyes were focused inward. She was not
in love with him after all, I told myself. He had been groping
her. She had gone to him because she was angry—because
she wanted some small revenge.

"I can't stay long," he said.

"You don't think Jake is actually on the run do you? I
mean, couldn't he just be out somewhere, for the evening?"
She was calm, full of the Southern willingness to be reasonable and hospitable, but beneath her decorum she was
afraid. I heard the shake in her voice, however slight, and
how her accent went soft, like it used to at night sometimes, lying beside me. "Part of me, I can't believe this is
happening."

"Don't worry."

She trembled again, more visibly now. She clutched herself and shivered on the tile floor. "What's the matter?"

"I don't have my slippers. Do you mind if I go get them?"

"No. I'll make you a drink, if you like."

"I was just having some tea—but all right. Pour me one."

Minor sauntered into the kitchen and emerged at the
other end of that room. I watched him through the open

archway. He pulled a bottle of J&B out of the cabinet and placed it on the counter. He turned my way then, square-shouldered and whistling like a fool, headed for the cocktail glasses in the living room hutch.

He did not see me at first. Then his posture stiffened and I felt things about to go haywire. I stepped forward with the gun pointed at his chest.

"Stay where you are."

I reached up under his jacket, patting him down, but I already had his gun. I'd taken it from his house. I made him take off the jacket altogether. I searched the pockets.

"I know what you're up to," I said, "the Liquid Ecstasy. Where is it?"

We stood in the living room, in the gloom. I caught our reflection in the window just behind him. There was a beam of light from the kitchen and Minor glowed a little bit in his white shirt. I stood like a shadow nearby, still wearing his clothes, the jacket I had taken from the closet, the tie. If anyone saw us from outside, they might easily mistake one for the other. I was Minor. He was me. So if by chance you could step outside this story, and see our images reflected in the window glass this moment, right now, you might be confused about which man it was who reached out then and put that small vial on the table. You might look from the reflections in the glass to the people standing before you and wonder whose hand it was that had snaked out of the darkness and left the bottle behind, and some of you might even believe the story the police tried to tell later: that it was I who'd brought the GHB, and Minor who'd tried to intervene.

"You killed Angela," I said. "You killed her and fixed the blame on Dillard. Then you killed Sara."

"You're crazy."

"You did the same with those other women, too, didn't you? Doping them up. Framing their lovers. Sometimes, you even got it to stick. Now you mean to do the same to Elizabeth. You mean to strangle her same as the others, and blame me."

"*It's you.*"

His voice was a whisper, so faint I wondered if he'd said anything at all, or if it was my imagination. He stood there like a stone, barely breathing, watching me.

"*You.*"

I laughed then. These psychopaths. Always switching things about. Corner them and they hold up a mirror. Try to blame the one who has discovered their crimes.

He looked at me as if I were the one who'd gone mad. As if I were the one whispering in the dark.

"Get on the floor," I told him, not knowing what I meant to do once I had him prone on the ground. Elizabeth would be back soon, and when she came I would have to do something. It would my word against his, her husband against this man on the floor—but I was in no way certain how she would choose.

"Get down."

He made a movement as if to comply, then suddenly swiveled his head. "Elizabeth," he yelled. It was a risky thing to do, I might have shot him, but instead I turned my head, looking, and in that instant he moved swiftly. He kicked the gun from my hand. I went after it, but he kicked it again, so it went spinning across the carpet, then he hit me hard in the face. My head snapped, I was stunned, and he plunged towards the cutlery table. I grabbed his hand. I tried to twist the knife away from him, but my footing was poor, and he forced me against the wall. I gripped his wrist. The blade was between us, in his hand, and I struggled to push it away.

Then I saw Elizabeth at the other end of the room. She was in a crouch, picking up the gun.

My hand slipped.

"Elizabeth," I gasped.

Whether she recognized the voice as mine, or his, I had no idea. It was an animal voice, full of pain. He had stabbed me, and in that instant time suspended itself. Minor and I stared into each other's eyes. He had his hand on the hilt. I felt my blood pulse. Across the room, the muzzle flashed in Elizabeth's hand.

Minor's back arched. He keeled away, turning towards Elizabeth. Then he stumbled to the floor. He ended on his back, halfway between us. I pulled the knife from my stomach and covered my wound with my hand. I moved toward my wife, out of the shadows.

"Elizabeth," I said again.

I could see the disbelief in her face

"No!" she cried

I took another step. Minor lay at my feet. The world was blackening.

"No!"

She had mixed us up. Me, in Minor's jacket, against the wall. Him, in his white shirt. She had confused us one for the other. I staggered toward her, bleeding, the knife still in my hand.

"No!"

She fired, point blank. Then she fired again. My body jerked. A wild flame burned inside my chest. I felt an excitement in my loins, the death excitement, I thought, I am dying. I fell down, on top of Minor, and the blade slipped through my fingers and onto the floor.

PART SIX

Incarceration and Trial

29.

I should be dead, I suppose. After all I was the criminal at large. I had been stabbed in the belly, then fired upon twice at close range. Even so, Minor's wound was through the heart, while my wounds, bloody and spectacular as they might have been, were not enough to carry me away. The one bullet had gone wide, the other lodged high in the shoulder. The knife wound had been more serious, but the county trauma unit had done a wonderful job. Minor, on the other hand, had been dead on arrival.

The police had come out to Golden Hinde the night of the shooting, but my memories of the shooting's aftermath are hazy and jump-cut. Dream images, almost. Minor lay dead beneath me. His lips were parted, his eyes open. Someone rolled me off him. They weren't too gentle about it, and I ended face up, with my hand across my stomach and the blood seeping through my shirt. Then a rescue squad burst through the door. They put me on a gurney, and I saw myself as if from above, my hands bloody, a froth at my lips, foamy and pink; meanwhile Elizabeth sat not far away, there on the sectional couch, hands between her knees. She was pale and calm in the way that people sometimes are when something terrible has happened. A cop leaned over her, trying to get some kind of statement.

They took her downtown later that night, I know. Though I wasn't there, I can imagine the scene well enough.

I can see Milofski in his rumpled shirt, and Elizabeth in her black pajamas, and Ted Hejl the lawyer by her side, with his suspenders and his cotton shirt and his accent carefully modulated to sound as if he were from nowhere at all.

What did she tell them?

The truth, I suppose.

That she'd seen two men struggling. That she'd shot Minor by accident, thinking he was the intruder. And when I stumbled from the shadows, holding the knife in my hand . . .

The memory grew more vivid. I stood with the family cutlery in my gut, looking into my wife's eyes.

Had she recognized me before she fired?

I could hear her voice telling them how she'd been afraid when she saw us struggling in the shadows. She hadn't known who was who, or even that the intruder was me. It was the same voice that had whispered to me hotly once upon a time, and the same voice, too, that had grown remote these last months, scolding me bitterly on the hillside

Another DA's office might have reacted differently, but in the end they had decided not to prosecute Elizabeth. She was the victim. A confused woman, acting in self-defense.

I was the one they wanted.

30.

On account of my condition, Jamie managed to secure me a room outside the county jail, in a private recuperation facility over in Ross. She kept me sequestered there. The police wanted to blame the shooting on me, as I have said, but it was difficult. It was clear I had not fired the gun. I was not trespassing—as it was my house, and there was no restraining order preventing me from being there. It wasn't even clear I'd been resisting arrest.

I lay recuperating for quite some time. There was a risk of an infection, and I ran one of those troubling fevers, on-again, off-again, that rose and peaked and vanished, only to return once more at the last moment, just as I was about to be taken to the county jail.

There was a television in the room, and also a telephone, and a cop outside the door. The nurses were frightened of me, but Jamie stopped by on a regular basis, and she stood by my bed when Milofski took my statement, making sure I didn't say anything I shouldn't. We played it pretty tight, and it got on Milofski's nerves—but my story was simple. That afternoon, when I'd disappeared from the apartment, I'd had no idea the cops were looking for me; no, I'd gone out to Golden Hinde to visit my wife. When she didn't answer, I went around back. I'd called out her name as I came in the door. Then Minor jumped me, thinking I was an intruder. We tussled in the dark and Elizabeth shot before the whole thing got sorted out.

When I was finished with my story, Milofski grinned. It was his bear grin, and it told me he wanted to grab me by the collar and throttle me and hiss in my face while I gasped for air.

"We found a bottle of Liquid X sitting on the table. Do you have any idea how it got there?"

I paused a moment. "I don't know what you're talking about."

"Did you come there with the idea of drugging your wife, and killing her, the same way you did Sara Johnson?"

Jamie interrupted. "You're straying into bad taste, Milofski. Our cooperation here is voluntary."

"Why did your wife shoot you, you think?"

"I don't know," I said. "The room was dark. Maybe she couldn't see too well."

"Yeah. Or maybe she don't like you so much."

Milofski started to laugh now, a noise that came from deep in his gut, and you could see in him his Russian ancestry, the Cossack giving some poor no-good a push in the belly, a little poke with the bayonet. He was just getting started, but Jamie cut him short.

"You can go," she said. "My client's told you all he can tell."

Jamie wore a red jacket with a velveteen collar, a

matching skirt, black boots. Milofski gave her the once over, hard and ugly, like he was on patrol and she was a whore on the street. "I don't think so," Milofski said. "He hasn't given me his little speech yet. How he's innocent, and the real killer's out on the street."

"Go," she insisted.

"What—and leave you two unprotected?"

"Get out."

Milofski left but he dallied outside the room, chatting it up with the cop on duty, telling him to shoot me if I tried to leave. He said it loud enough for me to hear. The cop guffawed, and Jamie closed the door. "You've made a mess of this," she said to me. "You should have turned yourself in, like I asked, rather than going out to your wife's place."

"I wanted to see her."

"Why?"

"Love, perhaps. She's my wife, after all."

"The GHB—what do you know about it?"

I hesitated. "They must have planted it out there—same as they planted it at my trailer."

Jamie didn't have anything to say to this. I considered giving her a more elaborate explanation, full of details: telling her I'd been out to Minor's house and seen the knock-out bottle, then driven out to Golden Hinde to save my wife. In the end, I decided no. I had no proof. Besides, if I changed my story now, even with my lawyer, it might only work against me.

Anyway I was not lying about why I had gone out to Golden Hinde. Not entirely.

"They've assigned a new prosecutor to the case," Jamie said. "Richard Sabel."

"I don't know him."

"He's new in the department. He's seeking to expand the indictment."

She wore a gaudy necklace and her hair hung loose and her eyes glistened in the dark room. She smiled oddly and her smile showed her teeth. I'd heard rumors about her private life, too, of course, the kind of rumors you might expect concerning a single woman in her profession. She was a lesbian. A nympho. She carried a knife in her purse.

"They've already got their evidence for the grand jury, for the murder and rape of Sara Johnson. Now they want to add new charges."

"They can't charge me with Minor's murder. I didn't even pull the trigger."

"Maybe not—but from what I hear there's a rumor going around that links you to some other strangulations around the state. Then there's the similarities between this and the Mori case. It's got people thinking."

She stood close by my bed, a little too close, smiling that odd smile of hers, regarding me with a certain affection, the way a young child regards an animal in a cage.

"It's all slander."

She shook her head and dropped her hand, fingers splayed, onto the white sheet: a dainty little hand, surprisingly so, with her nails painted rust—to match her hair, her lips—and an oversized bracelet dangling from her wrist.

"Perhaps, but the prosecution's added a new name on the witness list for the grand jury. A former patient of yours, Tony Grazzioni. Do you have any idea what that might be about?"

"No," I said.

She looked at me long and hard, as if she saw right through me, to the small lump of fear in my chest.

"Why do you do this?" I asked.

I put my hand on her hand. I was tempted to pull her towards me then. To feel her hard body with its limbs that were all angles and lines. To put my hand up her red skirt and stare into those black eyes. Meanwhile her hand moved underneath mine, and she looked at me as if I were something to be eaten and excreted. She had the purse over her shoulder and I imagined her reaching into that purse as I pulled her down, slitting me up the middle.

"Do what?"

"The work you do? Why?"

She grinned. She ran her eyes over my body and I felt low and vulnerable. I took my hand away.

"For the pleasure of a job well done."

Then she took a step away from the bed, and seemed to grow taller. She went on talking as if nothing had passed between us. "My guess, these new accusations, they're just so much noise. A way of drumming up some nasty press. Still, I don't want Sabel expanding the indictment. If successful, it gives him the opportunity to drag other evidence into the trial.

"I want to get this to trial quickly. They're bunglers up there in the DA's office. If we push them, they'll stumble. They'll contaminate the evidence just walking down the hall."

I nodded my agreement. It was a common enough strategy, and I did not catch at first the twitch in her expression, the small shift of the eyes that should have told me something else was coming, out of the ordinary. I touched the wound in my belly and ran my fingers through my hair, through the missing pony.

"To get us on the fast track, I had to make a compromise of sorts. I made an agreement with the judge. To a psychiatric evaluation."

"What?"

"Someone you know, I believe. Madison Paulie—he's going to talk to you on behalf of the court, to determine fitness to stand trial. I know this often takes place a little later, after the indictment has been finalized, but I agreed to let them talk to you now."

"I'm fit to stand trial. There's no question about that."

"Just talk to Mr. Paulie. He'll be along tomorrow."

"When's the grand jury meeting?"

"Next week."

"I don't like this."

"Just cooperate."

I tried to disagree, but her time was up now and she did

not intend to listen. When she left, I heard her heels clicking down the long hall. I imagined the cop watching her ass swing its way to the elevator, thinking his cop thoughts, despising her and wanting to fuck her at the same time. Maybe she'd even given him one of her hard-ass smiles, her Jamie Kaufman smiles, Queen of the Damned. Ugly, like I said, all angles and calculation, but not without her own kind of appeal. Still, I was wise not to have pulled her any closer. She might spring you, she might set you free, but for her own reasons. It made her feel powerful. It swelled her up, the idea of a guilty man out in the world, free by her doing. But move the wrong way, foul things up, she'd cut you to pieces, feed you to the swine. Innocent or no. Even so, she knew how to work the tabloids. She'd scolded me but the story of the lovelorn prosecutor, accidentally shot to death by his mistress, wife of the accused, it was everywhere now, and the prosecution's case was swamped in the backwash, in the flashbulbs and innuendoes, and Sabel was too new, too green, to fight her off. Or that's what I hoped, anyway.

31.

That night my fever returned. I had dreams, and in those dreams I divided into a hundred selves—and each of those divided into a hundred more—and one self was as innocent as could be, betrayed by his wife, framed by her lover—another was the man the prosecution claimed him to be: murderer, serial killer—another the poor boy raised in Baltimore, little boy Jake, poor Jake—still another walked by the marsh, wretched thoughts in his mind, the wind in his hair—danced in clubs, caught glimpses of himself in the mirror—while on the television other Jakes wandered in and out of living rooms—materialized in radio reports—in conversations—in the story I am telling now, to try and set the record straight.

By morning my fever had receded. Madison Paulie came to visit, as Jamie said he would. Paulie was dressed in a gray suit, but he still had the same scarecrow look, gangly and wild-limbed. His red hair was frayed and unkempt. His face was thin and pale, and the black mole on his cheek loomed larger, as if it had grown since the last time I'd seen him, at the Wilders' party. He had a way of regarding you, from the side, glancing away then back, that made it seem as if he were looking at you from two directions at once.

"How are you doing?" Paulie asked. His voice managed the sound of genuine concern.

"Not so bad."

I was suspicious. He'd been appointed by the court, and his findings would be open to the prosecution.

"You know the reason I'm here?" he asked.

I nodded, and he nodded, too. The nod of camaraderie. Shrink to shrink.

"I hear you grew up in Baltimore."

It was an effort to get me talking. I went along, telling him how I'd grown up in the row district down by the old stadium. I gave him my family background. I was careful the way I phrased things, but my mom and I, we were a social service case and there were records. He had access to them, I figured. Even if he didn't, he was savvy enough to guess the kind of details under the surface. Father who disappeared before I was born. Mother who tinted her hair a different color every week. A timid woman who had a secret love for things brutal and lurid. Who had trouble with little yellow pills that made her sleepy, and when she took them became amorous in a stupid, unconscious way. Men took advantage.

"I had a rocky childhood, I admit. Raised by a single mom, but she loved me. She did her best."

"Of course."

I could guess what he was thinking. My background matched the FBI profile for certain kinds of criminals. So did that of a lot of other people though. President Clinton, for example. Martin Luther King.

"You suffered from blackouts when you were a kid, didn't you? Sudden fits of rage."

"I outgrew it."

He nodded, made a note on his pad.

We were playing each other now. He wanted to draw me out, not caring so much what the subject matter was, just wanting to hear me talk, to listen to my associative banter and the kind of logical connections I made, so he could see if there were any indications of delusional thinking, or paranoia, or psychopathic manipulation of events.

"This has been hard on you, I imagine." His voice was sympathetic, and there was a blue glint in his eye. "The murder charges, all the publicity—it must be hard."

"It hasn't done wonders for my marriage."

"I'm sorry to hear that."

"We separated just before this happened, and . . . " I paused. "I'm sure you've read the stories in the paper."

"I don't imagine they are necessarily true."

"To be honest, it was good between Elizabeth and I for a long time. But more recently I don't know. . . . maybe it has to do with her father's death. Her expectations. . . ."

I put my head in my hand. Then a sound came out of me, from deep in my chest. The kind of solitary, wrenching noise you might expect from a man in my position, alone on a hospital bed, charged with murder, estranged from his wife.

He laced his fingers, wondering perhaps if the sob was real.

"You attended Chesapeake College, didn't you—for your undergraduate work."

"Yes, I did."

"You were there at the time of the Winkle murder."

I hesitated, taken aback at this sudden shift—but that's the way it was in my business. The talk always turned to murder. At any rate I knew the case. You couldn't have attended Chesapeake College when I did and not know. A co-ed, Karen Winkle, had been strangled to death in her room. They blamed the boyfriend for a while, but he had some kind of alibi, said she was into kinky sex with strangers, pushing the envelope. Some of her girlfriends said the same thing. Into popping, they called it then, asphyxiation as a way of heightening the orgasm. Walked around with rope burn on her neck, under the collar. Liked to pick up strangers. People speculated it was an incident of that type: a pick-up gone out of control.

"Why are you bringing this up?" I asked.

"In graduate school, I studied the case. Wrote a paper."

"What aspect did you study?"

"How the first time, for a serial murderer, it can set the pattern. It's not planned. It's something that happens in the course of another incident. The killer gets his first taste. After that, the events become more ritualized."

"I'm familiar with that phenomenon, yes."

"There were more deaths later, weren't there? A series of strangulations. Eventually, they arrested another kid at your college. He'd been dating one of the girls. Claimed he'd been framed."

"He was executed, if I remember."

"You were living with your mother at the time."

"Yes," I said, still agreeable, but I didn't much care for this line of questioning.

"Your mother died shortly after that, didn't she? A drowning incident. Same as your first wife."

"That's true."

"It must be hard for you."

"I don't follow."

"A number of women in your own life have died under unusual circumstances. Now—these allegations."

I understood what Paulie was doing. Trying to see if he could trace me back, establish a pattern that went deep into my past, knitting the events of my life together. Just doing his job, you might say, trying to see what he could see—but I didn't like it. I began to feel quite enraged. Then suddenly he stood up, glancing at his watch.

"Your doctor told me I could only have an hour today. He was quite firm. He doesn't want to wear you out."

"That all right. I don't mind talking."

"Don't worry," he said, and gave me a wink. "I'll be back in a few days."

32.

Something will happen, I thought. Something will come clear, some flaw will be found, and I will be set free. The next day, though, they transferred me over to the county jail. Jamie wasn't there this time; she let them take me unaccompanied. They handcuffed me in the back of a cruiser and drove me over, and once again I walked down that long corridor into the tombs. I was nobody in the tombs, just another prisoner. With each step, I felt myself disappear a little more. Inside my cell, the walls were gray and I knew it wouldn't be long before that grayness invaded my head. Images of the outside would come to me—my house, the sky overhead, a restaurant filled with people—and I would feel an anxiety, a sense of hopelessness. Some say it is the early days of incarceration that are the worst. After a while, the prisoner disassociates himself from his memories, and the outside world ceases to exist. It is a survival strategy, I suppose. If you don't learn it, you suffer. So it is best to be estranged, unattached, and let the memories drift by as if they belong to someone else.

Myself, I did not know if I could achieve that state. I am no aesthete. I am full of yearning.

I had a visitor.

The visitor was Nate Jackson, the detective, and he was the same as ever. Chinos and a polo shirt and his hair thinning across the top. He had the same sweet look as always, the same fat cheeks and mild, puzzled expression, and the same foul odor. He was nobody's fool though. He'd learned the hard way, I guess, the soft, fat kid on the school grounds, big but not strong, who kept the other kids off his case by knowing their secrets, the little things no one else knew. As long as you didn't cross him, he was your friend forever.

"What's up?"

"Remember, you asked me about Tony Grazzioni?"

"You found him?"

"Tahoe City. Down the other side of the lake. I got his address, you want it. Also the phone number of the people looking for him."

I was surprised sometimes how far out of his way he would go for me. What he owed me on account of his daughter, it was endless. Or that's the way he felt, it seemed.

"I appreciate the information, Nate."

"The tape," he said. "The one you made of my daughter, when you interviewed her out at Napa."

"I told you Nate, that's safe with me. It's confidential. Psychiatric privilege."

"Nothing in this world's confidential, you know that, Doc." His voice was soft and earnest. "Besides I got it on the inside the cops are looking to subpoena your files. I just can't risk them getting that tape."

"It's safe. Don't worry."

"Doc, if you don't give it to me. . . ."

It was the same voice, mellifluous and hypnotic as the late night rain pattering against a darkened window—but there was something else there, too. Nate's eyes went narrow. I thought he'd come out here to help me, but now I wondered. I'd seen this look once before, back when I first mentioned the tape to him—and the things his daughter had described.

"Just as soon as I get out of here. I'll get that tape for you. You can count on it."

Nate shook his head. He loved his little girl, that man, I have to say that for him.

"Let me tell you," he said. "I have an operative. Works out of Tahoe. He found Tony in one of those little casinos on the Nevada side. He couldn't resist the pull of the cards, that Tony. Anyway my guy struck up a conversation. He's a friendly son-of-a-bitch, my guy. Looks like nobody, loses at cards, listens good. So Tony loosens up. He starts talking about you, since you're all over the news. He says some things about you, some girls. . . ."

"No," I said, "Listen. . . ."

Nate held up his hand. "No," he said. "You listen." I heard the faintest rasp, something ugly and discordant that had been there all along, I supposed, beneath the surface. "This operative told me what Tony had to say about you. Then I went back to that scenario we constructed for Wagoner, and I thought how the wheels would start clicking in the DA's office if they heard Grazzioni talk. If somehow, some way, someone saw that document we prepared. They might start looking at some of those old cases. . . ."

"Come on," I said. "You're not buying into that. Grazzioni, he'd extort his mother if he could. If you're going to help the cops create a paper trail to prove his nonsense then . . . to say that I. . . . all those girls . . . ," I stammered, "then I don't know, I just don't know. . . ."

"Then there's the matter of the motel," he said. "And the man in the blue suit."

"I don't appreciate this kind of innuendo, Nate."

"Of course not. You know, I know, everybody in the world's got a blue suit. You. Me. General Eisenhower—all dressed up in his box there, under the ground. A detail like that, all alone, all by itself, it doesn't mean much."

His tone had turned nasty now. It was what made him a good investigator, I suppose, the ability to wrap his intentions in a sweet voice, then come after you full-throated, with a larynx full of pus. "Second time around, I sent a Spanish tongue to that motel," he said. "Someone a little better with the language than myself. Second time around our maid remembers another detail, about the way Mr. Blue

Suit wore his hair."

I touched the back of my head where the pony used to be. "The maid didn't say any such thing," I said.

He shrugged. "I want that tape."

He was bluffing. He had no proof, but it was the kind of thing people did when they found someone in my position, who could be easily bossed. I could call his bluff, but in the end he would do anything for his daughter. You couldn't blame him, I suppose. Either way it wasn't worth fighting him on this. So I told him where the tape was. I gave him the key code to my storage facility in Greenbrae. The police didn't know about it, not yet. The information seemed to take the edge off.

"Grazzioni is living in a condo with his brother," he told me. "Number fifty. North Shore Drive."

"What about the others? The ones he double-crossed."

"I have their phone number, too, if you want it."

I thought of the sky outside. I thought of the highway and the smell of leather upholstery and imagined a woman waiting for me somewhere, in a life up ahead. And I saw the road winding out of Marin, past all those beautiful brown hills, and for a second I was gripped by that horrible yearning—and a fear I would never escape.

"You call them for me, Nate. Tell them where Tony is."

We both knew what this meant. It wasn't hard to guess what Tony's old friends would do to him, given the money he owed. Nate looked offended at my request. He shook his head. "You're on your own. You want to make that call, you make it yourself."

I blinked. "Nate, please. It's not so easy for me to get to the phone here."

"I don't do that kind of thing."

"Getting kind of moralistic on me aren't you, Nate. I mean, given your daughter and all."

He fell quiet. His eyes were lost in the fat now, the lids all but shut, his nostrils widening, closing.

"I'm sorry Nate. I didn't mean anything. "

I had crossed the line and he sat there studying me, breathing heavily, judging whether he was going to forgive me. He was a hideous man really. His shirt was yellow with perspiration and his brow was damp. I could smell his foul odor despite the Plexiglas that kept us apart. He put his mouth up to the hole in the shield.

He whispered the number. I felt his breath through the hole. It stank of offal. Then he rose up, moist and rancid, an ugly mound of flesh, sweating his way across the jailhouse floor.

33.

The criminal imagines his victims, fantasizing, projecting, willing them into existence. I have read about this phenomenon in the psychiatric journals, and its opposite as well: about the victims who imagine their persecutor until at last, one day, the son-of-a-bitch appears.

Is the ultimate encounter by design then? Mutually created, by victim and criminal dreaming in concert? Or is it accident, fate, the random imposition of will by one human upon another?

I didn't know the answer, but a similar thing was happening to me, or so I felt: I was being imagined into my current existence, into this cell, by the mass who needed someone to blame, though in fact all they had against me so far were the usual sins. Shallowness, vanity, an obsession with the self. For most of them, though, these were good enough. I tried to escape the only way I knew, crossing my legs, imagining myself on the mountain. Meditating. All moments lead from this moment, I told myself, breathing deep. All possibilities, endless worlds, other lives. But when I opened my eyes I was still Jake Danser, still here, still in this cell.

34.

In the Marin County jail, the cells are grouped in pods, and each pod has its own common area. Everything in the pod is controlled electronically, and at certain times of the day the cell doors unlock, allowing you into the commons. I stood in line now waiting for my turn at the phone. I could see one of my fellow prisoners hunched in the phone booth on the other side of the surveillance glass. His ten minutes were all but expired. There were two more men in front of me. My fever had returned. My mouth was dry. My knees trembled.

I know what some of you are thinking. If I was innocent it wouldn't really matter. Let Grazzioni say what he wanted. Let him implicate me in every strangulation between here and Tehachapi, because when the circumstances were examined, Grazzioni's testimony would be revealed for what it was.

Only how could I be sure? Better men than myself have been put away with less cause.

The prisoner hung up. Another man took his place. I edged forward. He finished his call and I edged up again.

A guard tapped me on the shoulder.

"Your appointment's here. The psychiatrist."

"Can I make my phone call?"

"No."

"I've been waiting my turn here."

"Your turn is over," he said. "Come with me."

The guard escorted me down the hall to an interview room where Madison Paulie waited once again, smiling and affable, regarding me with the same half-turned head and quizzical glance as before, as if peering at me from around the side of a houseplant. He was an odd man. Curious about me, no doubt. Wondering if I was guilty. If my tears were feigned. If I was the man I seemed or some facsimile, some second image that reflected back onto the first. No matter, I wasn't insane by legal standards, surely he would see that. I was capable of standing trial and participating in my own defense. Ultimately that was all he had come to determine. But the conversation could go wrong, I knew. It could go wrong and I could end up at Napa or he could come to other conclusions that would send the case spinning in a direction I did not anticipate. So I had to be at my best.

"Last time, during our discussion, we touched on Blackout Syndrome. Do you remember?" he asked.

"Yes. I remember."

"Given your background, you must be familiar with the use of the term in criminal cases. Regarding patients who claim amnesia. Total loss of memory in regard to the crime itself."

His manner was more relaxed than last time, congenial in an off-hand way—as if the official part of the interview were over and we were just chatting now.

"I'm familiar with the syndrome. Or alleged syndrome, I should say."

"What's your opinion?"

He was flattering me, I knew, but I was willing to play along. "Most of them are malingering," I said. "Most of them are liars. But not all. Sometimes, if outside forces are powerful enough—the mind can be overwhelmed. Plummeted into darkness."

"Was that your opinion in the Dillard case?"

I shook my head. "That whole defense was misguided. An embarrassment."

"Yes, attorneys. They'll push the limits sometimes. Against our better instincts. It's an ethical dilemma—but let me tell you something." His eyes were earnest, fixated with a certain light. "I had a case not so long ago. It centered around a young man, a serial murderer. The evidence against him was overwhelming. He claimed he couldn't remember what he had done. Eventually he broke down in front of the jury, crying, full of remorse, as his memories swept over him in a flood. In the end, the jury sent him to an asylum."

"I have heard of such cases," I told him.

Like I said, I understood what Paulie was doing, talking to me on the professional level, flattering me up.

"You suffered from this syndrome yourself, I hear. Is that what drew you to the field?"

"Not so much," I said. "My condition, it was a childhood thing. Not what you're talking about at all."

"I've read the ambulance driver's report. He understood you to say otherwise."

"He misunderstood. What happened that day, it was an anxiety attack. I hyperventilated. Sara and I bumped heads. There was a lot of blood out my nose, but that's the nature of bloody noses. Sara called just to be safe."

He gave me his shrink face now, that placid veil: chin half-lifted; eyes in the ether—that benign expression that is supposed to give the patient license to talk, as if addressing some spirit in the underworld. I was tempted then to tell him about Minor Robinson. How he'd been shadowing me. Setting me up to take the blame, using rigged evidence and the testimony of a psychopath. I knew better though. Mad Paulie would think I was lying outright, or delusional. I didn't want either of those conclusions in his report to the court.

"During the mitigation hearings," Paulie went on, "I testified as to the veracity of his blackouts. I found his amnesia authentic. His violence, I determined, was repressed rage at the mother. Rooted in sexual abuse."

"Fascinating," I said.

"The last time you were with Sara Johnson, you remember every minute of it?"

I gave him a nod.

"You went out with her to the arbor, then followed her

across the lawn. You remember that, don't you?"

"Of course."

"Did you have a blackout later that evening?"

"No."

"Are you sure."

"Yes."

He smiled. The wide-eyed, lilting smile, bemused, weary. For a moment I felt feverish again, and his features seemed to elongate. I felt as if I were dividing into two, one part of me watching the other.

"I have a question for you, professional to professional," he said.

"All right"

"You've spent your life talking to criminals, just like I have. You've heard a million stories."

"That's true."

"So you're familiar with the violent impulse. It's deep-rooted in the brain. Though in some people, it's true, that impulse displays itself more than others."

"Yes."

"If we believe the Jungians, everything is born in its opposite. When a soul is out of balance, we nurture it with opposing elements. Beauty with violence, man with woman, fire with water. Opposites heal the psyche, move the individual toward self-integration. Though in the criminal population, such transcendence seldom occurs."

"No."

"Except, possibly, in the violent act itself."

He was appealing to my professional self again, or pretending to. It was one way to flush a psychopath into the open. Such individuals invariably regard themselves as more intelligent than anyone else. They like to play games. So one way to uncover them is to indulge their pretensions. String them along. Knowing this, I said nothing. I didn't think it wise. Paulie wanted to engage me. He was trying to draw me out, to get a glimpse inside of me, to see if in all of my manifold selves there was the one self he was looking for, and if I would somehow reveal it to him.

"The murderers I talk to," he said, "most of them, they don't fall to their knees tormented by guilt. No, far from it. They give you the big wink, the big smile. You've seen it, I'm sure: how they behave when they're escorted into the courtroom, in their bright orange suits. The arrogance. The sidelong smirk."

He was working me, like I said, or trying to work me, but I could also sense that this was not completely an act. These issues troubled him.

"When I first went into this field," he said. "I thought you could help individuals achieve spiritual balance. You could overcome the demons. It was a hard battle, I thought, but listening, talking, we make a contribution to criminology.

"After a while I came to look at it differently. There was just them over there, and us over here. Our job was to keep the door shut. Lock them away. Only they kept getting out. So I determined the function of our profession was something else altogether."

"What's that?

"We are conduits."

"I don't understand."

"By listening, we are letting the demons loose. We let them into the world. They spawn, multiply. Whisper in every corner."

In Paulie's face, I saw his own disturbance. Listening all these years, interviewing criminals—at some point it was as if he were no longer listening to someone else, but to a voice inside.

"You know that kid, I told you about? The blackout victim, the one they put in the asylum?"

"What about him?"

"They let him loose. He was a model patient. Sweet as hell. After a few years, they declared him cured."

"A happy ending?"

"He integrated himself into a new community. Remarried. Then it happened all over again. Three new victims. When they brought him in, it was the same story as before. He didn't remember."

"No?"

"I might have believed him, except for one thing. While he was out in the world, he confided in someone. Another con. In a bar. He told his buddy he remembered every minute. Every goddamn glorious minute. It was the pleasure of his life. You see, there'd been no amnesia. He knew exactly what he was doing. He'd fooled us all."

"So he's off the streets at least. He won't fool anyone again."

"No, I don't believe so."

"That's good."

"He was murdered in prison."

"I see."

"Castrated —with a razor. It happened in his cell."

I glanced inward now, and in that inner darkness I saw another self, bleeding to death on the prison floor. I touched my head. I was burning up.

"I'm innocent," I said.

He regarded me a long moment. "You look pale."

"I have a fever."

He came over and put a palm on my forehead. I looked at him and he looked back, and I could see him probing me. He was working on intuition. After the tests, the examinations, and our conversation, it all came down to this one moment. He realized, I'm sure, that I wasn't delusional. I was capable of standing trial. Even so he held his palm there a moment longer, trying to read my face, looking for that smile, maybe, for that small turn of the lips. Wanting to know something more. To get a glimpse way down into me. But whatever he saw, it was just himself, mirrored in my eyes. He took away his hand.

"You're burning up," he said. "I better call the guard."

35.

Fever overtook me once again, worse than before. I fell in and out of dreams, and in each one of those dreams, at the center of hell, was Tony Grazzioni, talking to the grand jury. *Yeah, yeah, the doc, he told me all kinda stuff. We shared confidences, you might say, and he told me some things. That woman in Vegas, strangled during the forensic convention, he knew the color of her blouse. The kind of pumps she was wearing.* Then I would wake up from this dream, in the jail infirmary, thinking I had to get to the phone, but it was night, it was dark. *The doc told me little details only an insider would know. Trying to draw me out, you know, like the shrinks do, tell you a little bit of theirs so you tell them a little bit back. Except he got carried away. Told me how in the beginning it was girls he didn't know, met in bars.* Then it was day, and I struggled up—but the nurse came, a male nurse, big as an elephant, and he put his hand on my forehead, forcing me back. Tony sat upright, naked from the waist up. His belly wiggled as he talked, like the words were emanating from his navel. *Later it was close to home. Women under his nose. Like Angela Mori. Acquaintance of mine saw them both together. Sold him some Liquid X down in SOMA.* Another morning, then night, then morning again. I was groggy. Someone poked me, jostled me awake. It was a mild-mannered little doctor who had the look of a torture expert.

"He was crying out all night," said the nurse.

"I need to make a phone call."

They ignored me. Grazzioni would testify soon, and I needed to get to the phone before that happened.

"Keep him another day," said the doctor. "He's still

feverish, and we don't want him dropping dead before he goes to court."

They gave me something to sleep and on the way under I caught a glimpse of Sara's face, and Angela's, and other women, too, a line that went back in time to the Winkle girl, but then all those faces vanished into flames, like pages in an incinerator.

Elizabeth. . . .

My fever had broken. For good, I hoped—but I still needed to get to the phone. The doctor felt my forehead, nodded. He gave his approval. The guards came and escorted me back to the pod.

That afternoon, I waited in line once more. Once more I watched the prisoners ahead of me, talking on the other side of the glass. I edged forward. The con in front of me hung up. A guard passed.

My turn.

I dialed the number Nate Jackson had given me.

"Who is this?"

I closed my eyes. If I had an ounce of misgiving, it was here, now. Or maybe it was pleasure. I closed my eyes and saw him inside me then, that greedy fuck staring into the void, sucking me in. Insatiable.

"I knew where Tony is," I said. "Tony Grazzioni, I can tell you. But if you want him, you better move fast."

36.

Monday was Tony's day in front of the Grand Jury, but he didn't show. Not that day, not the next. Not until two weeks later, when a water skier up at Tahoe hit something soft and ungainly out in the middle of the lake. By that time, the grand jury had made its decision. And Jamie was right. The DA's office bungled its presentation. The prosecution failed to expand the charges against me—and the indictment was limited to the murder and rape of Sara Johnson.

37.

The official trial is a matter of public record, and there are many of you, I am sure, who know the outcome, and have some idea of my own fate, and of what happened to Elizabeth later, after this was all over, when she fled to that little cottage she'd always wanted, down in Tomales Bay, with the steps down to the water, and no prison on the other side. Still I know that events such as these slip quickly from the public consciousness, and there are some among you, I imagine, who know nothing of the trial at all.

There is much that I could relate. I could for example create a picture for you of Richard Sabel. A blonde, punchless man in his mid-thirties, full of ambition. Forever waving his arms, forever glowering. I could tell you, too, how I sat at the defense table, listening in silence to his accusations while Queen Jamie sat beside me, businesslike in her high-collared blouse and her gray jacket, with her russet hair pulled back and that hard smile on her face.

I could recreate for you as well the lurid atmosphere of the trial. The morgue photos Sabel projected onto the courtroom wall. Sara full-length, Sara up close, Sara in extremis. The string of confidantes Sabel called to the stand. All with their stories to tell, implying my pursuit of Sara had been full of ill intent from the beginning. This followed by endless experts—blood, saliva, skin—leading up to the DNA specialist, a squirrelish little man whose testimony was filled with charts and calculations, a recitation of probabilities—a million to one, a billion—all indicating, yes, the sperm inside Sara Johnson belonged to me, Jake Danser, and no one else.

Yes, I could relate all this to you, and the feeling of doom that overcame me, and how that feeling did not abate even as Queen Jamie launched my defense. I could tell you how she maneuvered to make this trial about Minor Robinson rather than me. How she recalled Milofski to the stand, and got him to admit the irregularities in the searching of my trailer. And how Lady Wilder told the jury, in her recollection, no I had not been wearing a tie when I left her party—but yes, she had seen Minor Robinson poking around the arbor after I'd gone. I could relate all of this to you, but in the end it is simple prelude. Because it was only Elizabeth that mattered. Only my wife, and her testimony before the court.

Elizabeth entered the courtroom that day wearing a gray jacket with black lapels, a matching skirt, a white blouse. She had a classy air about her, demure and elegant, but there was also the air of scandal. I felt a small rush as she walked by. I could smell her fragrance, hear the rustle of her skirt. She didn't glance in my direction. She took the oath, and the jury heard for the first time her backporch drawl, the jasmine in her voice, the cobbler mixed in there with the East Coast education, and they wondered, I guess, at the truth behind the news stories. How this woman with the proud manner, the expensive clothes and the flame white hair—a handsome woman, a scholar, a person of means and intelligence—how she could have gotten herself at the center of such a mess.

"How long have you been married to the defendant?"

"Three years."

"Happily?"

The line of her jaw tightened with disdain. "We were happy for a while."

"You separated recently, is that true?"

"Yes."

"Were you seeing anyone else during this time?"

"Objection!"

Throughout the trial, Jamie had been doing her best to provoke Sabel—with her constant insinuations against Minor Robinson. The prosecutor was quick to jump up in outrage. Now the two attorneys approached the bench. There was some heated whispering. Meanwhile Elizabeth sat quietly. She wore her father's pearls, as always. I know I have mentioned them more than once, how her father had given the pearls to her as a way of claiming her forever, and there were times, I admit, when I'd felt like yanking them from her neck.

"The night of the party at the Wilders'. What time did you arrive?"

"At about nine. Maybe a little after."

"Did you come alone?"

"Yes. I took a taxi."

"Why a taxi?

I leaned forward in my seat and felt the eyes of the jury on me. At stake here were two versions of the truth. One in which I'd drugged and strangled Sara with my necktie in her apartment. Another in which I was the victim, a betrayed husband framed by an overzealous prosecutor.

"The reason I took a taxi . . ." Elizabeth faltered, her face blossoming a sudden red. "I didn't want to worry about driving home later, after a couple of drinks. I don't like to drive if I've been drinking."

"Did you expect to meet Minor Robinson at the party?"

"Objection!" Sabel took to his feet again.

"Nonsense," said Jamie. "The prosecution introduced the subject of the party, including the matter of Minor Robinson's presence there. It is well within our purview to pursue this matter."

"Objection overruled," said the judge. "The witness will answer the question."

"I was aware of the fact Minor might be there," said Elizabeth.

"In fact—didn't you meet him out front, and walk in together?"

"We bumped into each other."

"Did you talk to your husband inside the party?"

"Briefly."

"What did you talk about?"

"He wanted to know if I had come alone. Or with Minor Robinson."

"What did you say?"

"Alone. I told him I had come alone."

"When in fact you had come with Minor Robinson?"

"No. I ran into Minor out front. It wasn't planned."

"But you went home together?"

"He gave me a ride."

"What time was that?"

"About midnight."

"Did he come inside?"

"No."

The little rush in my heart grew faster, more erratic. I wanted to believe Elizabeth and Minor had not been together. Not that night, or any other. I wanted to believe despite what I myself had seen from the shadows at Golden Hinde, and despite the fact that the more unfaithful she'd been, the more wanton, the more it helped my case. She glanced at me then. The jury saw. It was the briefest of glances, but our eyes met and held, and in that instant it was as if we regarded one another from trawlers unhinged at sea, the chasm between us grower wider with each passing instant, the water colder, deeper.

"At the party, you saw your husband with Sara Johnson?"

"I caught a glimpse of them, dancing."

"Did you see them go out to the arbor together?"

"I heard about that later."

"Were you aware of the fact that Minor Robinson went out to the arbor, after your husband had left."

"No," said Elizabeth.

"Now, the coroner has established the time of Ms. Johnson's death between one A.M. and four A.M. Was Mr. Robinson with you during the hours in question?"

"Objection!" Sabel exploded. He was standing now and his yellow hair was straight up in the air, like a figure in a cartoon. "This line of questioning is designed to implicate the prosecutor. It is unseemly. The prosecutor was killed in the line of duty. He is not on trial here."

Jamie gleamed. In his righteousness, Sabel had voiced out loud the point she'd been trying to make through insinuation. Minor had visited the arbor after Sara and I. Perhaps he had found the tie I'd left behind. Then, between the hours of one and four. . . .

"Overruled," said the judge. "Answer the question, please."

"No. He was not with me. I don't know where he went."

The examination went on. Sabel fought every question, but Jamie was relentless. She asked Elizabeth about other times she and Minor had gotten together. For coffee in San Rafael. After the conference in Sonoma. At the Racquet Club. The movies.

I listened with the dread of a jealous husband, humiliated, feeling the heat rise in my cheeks.

The judge had prohibited cameras, but the reporters were here. Studying me, studying Elizabeth. Scribbling their observations. Like everyone else, I'd been following the newspapers, and I knew how absurd those observations could be. The case had been magnified, presented as an example *au courant*, reported not only for its own sake but used by editorialists to berate anything that needed berating. The criminal justice system. The efficacy of modern psychology. New Age religion and the lifestyles of the middle-aged. There was, of course, the inevitable analysis in the Sunday supplement. You can almost predict the words, I am sure: how the trial was more than a trial—a window into society at large and the way we live today.

We are too concerned with the surface of things. Accumulation for accumulation's sake. We fail to see what lies beneath. We move from thing to thing, person to person, belief to belief. Materialism is the spirituality of the

New Age, cloaked in self-help, in psychology, in a pan-religious Unitarianism that ignores the real demons within.

To fill that emptiness, the writers concluded, we consume. Not just objects, but each other as well.

Nonsense, of course. I'm sure you agree.

The kind of babble you might expect from a freelance journalist in the Sunday supplement. Nonetheless, the writers were still here, scribbling away, and we were impressed by their presence. Elizabeth's testimony continued. Jamie asked her about a night she and Minor had gotten together at Golden Hinde, not long after I was brought in for questioning.

"What was the subject of that conversation?"

"Minor was worried. The evidence against Jake, he said it looked pretty bad."

"What was your reaction?"

"I didn't know what to think."

"Did it ever occur to you that he was trying to remove your husband as a rival?"

She hesitated. "No."

"Did you believe the case against your husband, when Minor first told you?"

"Not at first."

"But later you did?"

"I began to wonder."

"In other words, the more intimate you became with Minor Robinson, the more you doubted your husband's innocence."

Sabel jumped to his feet. "Leading the witness."

"Sustained," said the judge.

Elizabeth's composure had diminished. Her blush had begun to deepen but it wasn't a pretty blush. It made her face look raw. She still had her beauty, more or less—but her white hair under the courtroom light had lost its platinum sheen. It no longer seemed dramatic but rather colorless and frayed. She touched the pearls about her neck. It was a small gesture, one that I'd seen many times—a simple flourish, the kind that wealthy girls make, with bluing in their blood—but at the moment the elegance was gone and she seemed fragile and a little bit old.

"Mrs. Danser," Jamie asked, "did it ever occur to you in regard to Mr. Robinson, that your friendship—as you refer to it—and his role as prosecutor, that these two things might put him into conflict?"

"It made for a conflict in us both, I think."

"Yet you continued to see him, even though he was prosecuting your husband."

"He came by the house a couple of times. To talk."

"About what?"

I could sense her weakening. If I could have gone to her then and erased everything that happened—and returned to that moment in her convertible, to that halting look in her blue eyes—I might have done so. "After the lab evidence came in, Minor was more and more convinced that Jake was the killer. He was worried for me. He was concerned, about what Jake might do."

"Were you in love with Mr. Robinson?"

"We had friendship that went back a number of years."

"Friendship?" Jamie's voice inflected higher, and her face lit up. "Was it this friendship that inspired him to come out to Golden Hinde on the evening of the 29th? The evening he was shot and killed."

Elizabeth's lips quivered and her eyes misted and I thought for a moment she might collapse into tears.

"Come now, the police have cleared you of all charges. Tell us what happened."

"Jake had disappeared," she said. "Minor was worried he might come by the house. He was concerned for my safety."

They went over the evening again, detail by detail. Minor knocking on the door. The scuffling in the shadows. The gun on the carpet. How Elizabeth, in the darkness, could not recognize for certain which of us was which.

"When you shot Mr. Robinson, who did you think he was?"

"I didn't know."

"Please, Mrs. Danser. You must have had some thoughts in your mind. When you pointed that gun, you had two figures to choose from."

"I was confused," she said. "Minor and my husband, they have similar builds. Minor had taken off his coat, but I didn't know that. All I saw was the white shirt. I thought maybe Jake, or someone else, I don't know who, had broken in somehow. And when I saw the man in the white shirt, pressing the other man against the wall—when I heard him cry out, I fired."

"So you shot him?"

"Yes."

"And when it turned out you were mistaken, and you saw Minor Robinson on the floor, and your husband emerged from the shadows, what did you do?"

Elizabeth looked resigned. She was undone. Jamie had gotten her to pay for my defense, then double-crossed her, releasing information about her and Minor, turning her life into a tabloid affair for the sake of my defense. Now Jamie sought to humiliate her in the courtroom.

"I shot him," she said, with the faintest of smiles. "Twice. But as you can see, he refuses to die."

There was laughter in the courtroom. I might have laughed, too—if it had been some other man's wife up there, and she were talking about someone other than myself.

"Mrs. Danser, were you having an affair with Minor Robinson?"

"Objection."

"Overruled. The witness will answer the question."

Elizabeth glanced at me as if from the bottom of the sea, her eyes glassy, remote. The truth was going to come out now. I had been cuckolded. I saw sorrow in her aging face, and grief—and a dark expectancy, too.

The judged prodded her again. Jamie repeated the question.

"Were you having an affair with Minor Robinson?"

"Yes," she said at last.

She said it proudly, and with malice, and her expression reminded me of how she had looked that day out on the cliff when I'd realized she meant to end it between us. My affair with Sara, she meant to hold it bitterly in her heart. I felt my own anger now. Maybe it was not reasonable, but I could not help feeling that if she had not pushed me away, that night at the Wilders' party, I would not have pursued Sara. This trial would never have taken place.

I am innocent.

Queen Jamie pressed on. She had the angle she wanted. She puffed herself up, slatternly with indignation.

"Are you telling me, Mrs. Danser, that you were sleeping with the prosecuting attorney. The man who was manipulating evidence against your husband—"

"Objection! Leading the witness."

"Sustained."

"The same man who went back to the arbor to gather the silk tie."

"Objection!"

The judged rapped his gavel. "Order!" he snapped.

"The same man who—"

"Objection!"

The judge gaveled her down. "Ms. Kaufman, be quiet! And stay quiet! Or I will cite you for contempt!"

Finally Queen Jamie obeyed. The judge ordered her last remarks stricken from the official record. Jamie stood chafing, pacing, angry, but it was all calculated, part of the show. She had accomplished what she had meant to accomplish. The jury knew what she wanted them to know. The former prosecutor had been sleeping with the defendant's wife. And all the evidence against me was tainted by this simple fact.

What follows, it seems like a dream, and in that dream, I see the last days of the trial, and the faces of the jury, and feel again the swings of emotion. I see Sabel, too, delivering his final statement, repeating the evidence in his slow, methodical way, building towards the moment when he would point in my direction, and ask the jury to convict me for the murder of Sara Johnson. Then it was Jamie's turn, summarizing our case, explaining again how I had walked out to the arbor that night, and made love to Sara, and left behind my tie. I was an innocent man, guilty of indiscretions, yes, she admitted, but were these any worse than the indiscretions committed by the deceased prosecutor? Whose hands were all over the evidence, guilty of the baldest of manipulations, for the basest of motives? How could you trust the evidence gathered by Mrs. Danser's illicit lover? What kind of justice is this? she asked, and at some point in this memory, this dream, I see the jury file out. I am alone in my cell. My heart races. The walls are gray, and I can see myself disappearing into that grayness, down long corridors into days that are yet more gray and in that grayness the jury returns. The foreman stands, reading the crimes of which I am accused. A woman on the jury gives me an unhappy smile. Then the verdict itself, the rush of noise, the gargled cry of Sara's boyfriend, the disbelieving sobs of her relatives, cries of injustice—Jamie embracing me meanwhile, an embrace like the devil's, spider-like and cold—and the video strobe in my face. On the courthouse steps, Jamie speaks for me, pushing back the crowd, insisting I am too exhausted to make a statement, saying this has been very hard on me, but now is the time for healing, and at this I bow my head, moving toward the waiting car, but not before a smile washes over my face, and the tears well up, and ten thousand shutters snap all at once—and it is that picture I see the next day on the tabloid, the smile together with the gleam in the eye, the smirk, that photo underneath the headline: PSYCHO SHRINK GOES FREE.

Epilogue

38.

I have rebuilt my life. I know there are people whose blood curdles at the thought. Who believe I have gotten away with murder. Not just of Sara but also of Angela Mori. And others, they say now, compiling a growing list. Blaming me for every corpse in a wayside ditch.

After the trial, I tried to stay on in Marin, but I was too much recognized. Vilified in convenience stores. Spat upon by women with remade breasts and dyed blonde hair. People would slow down their white sedans and point at me as I walked under the pepper trees. It was a hard bit of ignominy, but there were others also who sought me out. Men who clapped me upon the back and women who, when they saw me in the supermarket aisle, suddenly became wide-eyed and flirty.

I was photographed in nightclubs. I was seen dancing, drinking, dating. There are those who say I stayed in my old haunts to rub my nose in the justice system, to pose in front of the cameras, to mock. To torment poor Elizabeth. But that is unkind. I'm aware that there were those, after the trial, who wanted to reopen the case against her. For the death of Minor Robinson, for my shooting. But the DA's office declined—it was too great a reversal to go after her now. I am aware, too, of the fact that Elizabeth moved from the area, and of what happened to her afterwards. Or of the stories anyway. The house on Tomales Spit. The abandoned dinghy. The man who rented it, under an assumed name, and disappeared.

Some people are cursed. There are people whom the devil follows. Given all that has happened, I suppose it is inevitable that certain rumors would circulate. That these rumors would say I was the unidentified man. The one people saw in the darkness that day, on the waterfront, up there on the sand on Tomales.

The truth is, I had resettled long before her disappearance. I lived an itinerant life for a while, I admit. I changed my name, my looks. I took up residence in old hotels, but eventually I found a new life, in a new town. I pulled myself together.

For obvious reasons, I cannot tell you the name of that town. I do not want my alleged crimes to haunt me. I can tell you, though, that in many ways—the most important ways, perhaps—the place where I live now is not so far from where I lived before. I can create for you the general shape of my life now, the truth of things, even if in the interest of this truth there are certain details I must alter. Such is often the way with truth. The facts are not wide enough to contain it.

I don't think I risk my identity too much if I tell you I am remarried. In the town where I am living, there is a college nearby. I have found myself a new career, lecturing to students, undergraduates in the field of psychology. I have always been able to speak well, and though I started out as an adjunct, it wasn't too long before I had earned myself a small place on the faculty here. I should tell you, too, that the years have not been unkind to me. I am a decade older—and I have thickened as men do—but though my face carries the marks of its hardship, it carries, too, the look of experience. I have grown into my new role, taking on the look of a college professor, with my jacket, my glasses and my well-trimmed beard.

I still, sometimes, wear my hair in a pony.

I have stepped into my new life as onto a stage, I admit, but I enjoy it. I enjoy, too, those young eyes watching me at the lectern, as I pose and ponder, as I remove my jacket, roll up my sleeves, write on the blackboard the name of the class:

The psychology of the self.

I look about earnestly, and the earnest young eyes look at me full of expectation.

This new existence, I have not achieved it alone. It wasn't too long after I found my way here that I met up with my new wife. She is a beautiful woman, and there are times when it seems this is the only life I have ever lived. She has just turned the corner on fifty, and I am not so far behind. She has three children who are grown. Her clothes are stylish and her hair is colored in such a way as to resemble a sun-drenched version of its former self. On the refrigerator there are pictures of the two of us together, on vacations to the kind of places people like us go. Tuscany, maybe. Or Sao Paulo. Or one of those beaches on the backside of the Big Island, away from the tourists. We lounge in our polo shirts and our shorts, mug for the camera, put our hands around each other's waists. We smile. Also, on that same refrigerator, are the pictures of her kids and their families, children and grandchildren. They are like my own now. A couple of times a year, they make it home, gathering around the table for the feast, and the children grab me about the knees and call me grandpa.

So I have left the past behind as well as I could. Part of it lives there in the darkness, in my memory, but those memories are for me alone. If my wife wonders about my life before we married, she doesn't ask—just as I don't ask her. She has her photographs in her albums, of course, but they are but thin manifestations, images between bound covers there on the bottom shelf.

In many ways my life perhaps is not so different than yours. I have my routine, my work to do. I drive down our tree-lined street, through the neighborhood, across town. I walk across campus. My office is lined with books, with Freud and Hillman and Jung and Rank, case studies of this and that, deviance, brain disease, sexual insatiability, and when my students come to visit they glance about at all these books as if they are doorways into the unknown. I linger in the halls here. I talk to my colleagues. (I am well-liked, but there is one here who despises me. There is always one. He fought my appointment, cast aspersions on my scholarship, resists my promotions. The simple explanation: he is envious of my success. Of my wife, too, I suspect. But, as I said, there is always one like him, one such shadow.) I go about my business. I walk down the hall to the class where the light comes pouring through the windows like something in a sunlit dream.

I write on the board:

Who are you?

I smile, and the kids look about at each other, confused. Then I explain to them. It is a game. I invite the kids to play, to peel back the onion, all of our multiple selves, until eventually we come to that frightening part that lives in each of us. I look at a young woman in the front row, leaning on her elbows, hanging on to every word. Sometimes she comes up to me after class. I have seen her lingering—off the main path, in the daffodils, in her plaid skirt, her white blouse, her black boots.

In every life there are certain patterns, certain things that get repeated,

A while ago, I contacted Nate Jackson, the private detective. He was surprised to hear from me, but he talked in the old congenial way. His daughter had had more trouble, it seemed—and had moved to Europe, across the sea.

"That's too bad," I said. "There's a small matter, I wanted to clear up. The tape."

"Oh, I got it, doc. It was right where you said."

"Good, good. It turns out, there's a duplicate."

There was silence now, a little awkward. I heard that breathing of his, and imagined his wide cheeks. Did he think I had withheld it on purpose? I didn't want him to believe this. So I told him I'd be glad to send it to him. There was just a small favor he could do.

Go out into the marsh. To the wooden pier. Take five steps east. Then dig.

He obliged me. It's funny the ties that bind us to people you would not expect.

As soon as I received the box, I took it down into the basement. The lock was rusted, and I had to break it—but the contents were pretty much unchanged. I looked through it all. The button of a skirt. A debutante's ring. The earring I had taken from Sara on our last meeting. A dozen items like this, two dozen. Collected over time.

All of these were things I had once hoped to bury, but now I realized the folly of it. Because there is always one more thing to bury. We are never done. The reason I wanted the box, I had some mementos to add. New things I won't mention—another earring, perhaps, a skirtband—but also a certain necklace, with pearls the size of a child's teeth. So when the box came, I took it downstairs. There was a loose stone—a brick to pull out, and I put new memories inside that little box, and shoved the entire collection into the damp hole behind that loose brick. I go back on occasion, down to the basement, and fumble longingly. Maybe add something more.

Elizabeth, I think, *My poor Elizabeth.*

I go upstairs. Mary, I see, is waiting. She has her hands on her hips, but she gives me a kiss. Somewhat reluctantly, I admit. We are no longer in that phase of our marriage where we touch and fondle at the slightest impulse. Today she looks at me with something like skepticism. Our ardor for one another has cooled. It is inevitable, I guess.

"Where were you?" she asks.

"In the basement. Tinkering."

"No, I mean before that."

"At school."

"I stopped by your office, but I couldn't find you anywhere."

"I had to go over to the bookstore. There's a problem with the text I ordered for my class."

"Did you get it fixed?"

"No, of course not. You know that place. I was there all morning—and I never did find the right person in the bookstore."

"Oh," she says. "Well I hung around your office for quite a while."

"I'm sorry, honey," I say.

I come up behind her. We regard ourselves in the hall mirror, and meanwhile I run my hand under her waistband, down into her pants. All this seems to make her feel better, though I can see she is still a little bit disgruntled, ill at ease.

"Let's go out to dinner," I say.

She agrees. We go out to one of the nicer places—the type of place where they bring the visiting professors, the deans, the research specialists. I see my colleague there, the one who despises me. I stop to banter nonetheless. We discuss department business. His eyes gleam. Then the talk turns, as it does these days, to the most recent murder. A coed, this one. The talk dies away. Later, my wife and I are hand in hand, coming up the walkway, back to our house.

"I saw her picture, the red hair—the white slacks. She was such a self-assured girl. With such a future. Who would ever think."

"I don't know."

"The boy they arrested, he denies it," she says.

"They always deny it," I say.

Then we go inside, and she lies there quietly, and if there are shadows in that darkness, I don't know, if people disappear into other lives and come back and disappear again, I don't know that either, but suddenly I am aware of my wife, lying there beside me, and I decide that I must possess her and I do so, taking her roughly (onto her stomach, she moans, not used to this, no, please, she says, but there is ecstasy in her pleading), and for a minute everything disappears into the darkness, and then we are left, lying there, out of breath in the moonlight, exhausted, spent, and my wife sobs.

Then the next morning it is light—a wild, delicious light—and I am back in front of the classroom, where they are all listening to me, mouths open.

Who are you?

The students gather around me, and in their gathering I can sense their futures, their lives. We are talking about the psychopathic image. About death. About rape and murder. The class scintillates.

"Ritual," says one. "The grizzly crime, the corpse. It's a social ritual. Goes back to Jack the Ripper."

"It's like Jung says. The world is made of opposites. You can't have the light without the dark. You need it to be whole."

"We need the face of death in our lives, dream images, the grotesque."

"Most of the time, we can't deal with the truth. We black it out."

"Or we pretend to black it out."

"I don't like this conversation at all," says another. "Not one bit. I feel like I am being manipulated."

Through all this I say nothing, silent as a Buddha. The wind is quiet. The young woman I mentioned earlier, she has a seat in the front row. She smiles, I smile back. I walk from the classroom. Feel the bright light of the morning. I remember for a moment how I stood on a far-away street, looking down at the water, the empty house with the light on, and I can taste the essence of that moment—the evergreens, the dark scudding clouds, the mountain looming behind, waiting—even now as I walk across the campus, under sycamores, toward the hillock where the young coeds smile and lounge. As I approach, hearing them giggle, there is still another part of me looking down at that empty house, holding the necklace in my hand, the pearls, listening to the knock of that boat against the dock, the sound floating over the darkening sea, hearing it inside me, like the knocking of my heart. *Poor Elizabeth.* Meanwhile, the day is bright all around me. I turn away and walk down the long knoll to where the young woman leans against the tree, standing there in the bed of blooming flowers. *Later, you and me.* I whisper. I give her a wink. She smiles and bends my ear to her mouth, touches it with her tongue. In the distance stands my colleague. Looking at me with scorn, desire. He thinks he knows all of my secrets—and I know his. And for a moment, it's as if I am him and he is me, and the two of us, we turn away, then turn back, beneath the trees, in this dappled light. We circle each other on the path.

Lawrence
BLOCK
Grifter's Game

Originally Published As 'MONA'

Con man Joe Marlin was used to scoring easy cash off gullible women. But that was before he met Mona Brassard — and found himself holding a stolen stash of raw heroin. Now Joe's got to pull off the most dangerous con of his career. One that will leave him either a killer — or a corpse. GRIFTER'S GAME was the first mystery novel multiple Edgar Award-winnner Lawrence Block published under his own name. It is now appearing for the first time under his original title.

"[The] one writer of mystery and detective fiction who comes close to replacing the irreplaceable John D. MacDonald."
— STEPHEN KING

Order at www.HardCaseCrime.com or call 1-800-481-9191 (10am to 9pm EST)
...Or Mail in This Handy Order Form:

Dorchester Publishing Co., Inc., P.O. Box 6640, Wayne, PA 19087-8640
5349-7 $6.99 U.S. ($8.99 Canada)

Please add $2.50 for shipping and handling for the first book and $0.75 for each book thereafter. NY and PA residents, please add appropriate sales tax. No cash, stamps, or C.O.D.s. All orders shipped within 6 weeks via postal service book rate. Canadian orders require $2.50 extra postage and must be paid in U.S. dollars through a U.S. banking facility. Payment must accompany all orders.

Name _____

Address _____

City _____ State _____ Zip _____

I have enclosed $ _____ in payment for ____ copies of this book.

Fade to
BLONDE

by MAX PHILLIPS

Ray Corson came to Hollywood to be a screenwriter, not hired muscle. But when a beautiful girl with a purse full of cash asks for help, how can you say no?

Rebecca LaFontaine came to Hollywood to be an actress, not a stag movie starlet — or a murder victim. To protect her, Corson signs on with dope king Lenny Scarpa. But Scarpa, he finds, is hiding dark secrets. *And Rebecca's hiding the darkest secret of all…*

PRAISE FOR THE NOVELS OF MAX PHILLIPS:

"*A rip-roaring page-turner.*"   New York New·
"*Vividly written… Highly entertaining.*" — Kirkus   ·vs
"*A graphic satire of bedroom mores.*" — The New Yorker
"*Stunning.*" — Daily Mail (London)

Order at www.HardCaseCrime.com or call 1-800-481-9191 (10am to 9pm EST)
…Or Mail in This Handy Order Form:

Dorchester Publishing Co., Inc., P.O. Box 6640, Wayne, PA 19087-8640
5350-0 $6.99 U.S. ($8.99 Canada)
Please add $2.50 for shipping and handling for the first book and $0.75 for each book thereafter.
NY and PA residents, please add appropriate sales tax. No cash, stamps, or C.O.D.s. All orders shipped
within 6 weeks via postal service book rate. Canadian orders require $2.50 extra posta   be
paid in U.S. dollars through a U.S. banking facility. Payment must accompany all orders.

Name _____

Address _____

City _____ State _____ Zip _____

I have enclosed $ _____ in payment for ____ copies of this book.

ERLE STANLEY
GARDNER
TOP OF
Writing as
'A. A. Fair'
THE HEAP

When a gangster's beautiful girlfriend vanishes, the last man to be seen with her goes to P.I. Donald Lam for an alibi. But the client's story doesn't add up, and soon Lam's uncovered a mining scam, an illegal casino, a double homicide, and a chance for an enterprising private eye to make a small fortune — *if he can just stay alive long enough to cash in!* The return of the legendary, long-out-of-print Cool & Lam mystery series from the creator of Perry Mason.

"The best-selling author of the century… a master storyteller."
— The New York Times

FIRST PUBLICATION IN OVER 30 YEARS!

Order at www.HardCaseCrime.com or call 1-800-481-9191 (10am to 9pm EST)
...*Or Mail in This Handy Order Form:*

Dorchester Publishing Co., Inc., P.O. Box 6640, Wayne, PA 19087-8640
5352-7 $6.99 U.S. ($8.99 Canada)
Please add $2.50 for shipping and handling for the first book and $0.75 for each book thereafter. NY and PA residents, please add appropriate sales tax. No cash, stamps, or C.O.D.s. All orders shipped within 6 weeks via postal service book rate. Canadian orders require $2.50 extra postage and must be paid in U.S. dollars through a U.S. banking facility. Payment must accompany all orders.

Name _____

Address _____

City _____ State _____ Zip _____

I have enclosed $ _____ in payment for _____ copies of this book.

Little Girl Lost

by RICHARD ALEAS

Miranda Sugarman was supposed to be in the Midwest, work-ing as an eye doctor. *So how did she wind up dead on the roof of New York's seediest strip club?*

Ten years earlier, Miranda had been P.I. John Blake's girlfriend. Now he must uncover her secret life as a strip tease queen. But the deeper he digs, the deadlier the danger... until a shattering face-off in an East Village tenement changes his life forever.

LITTLE GIRL LOST is the stunning debut novel from Shamus Award-nominated RICHARD ALEAS, a writer whose stories have been selected for *Best Mystery Stories of the Year*. It features a brand new cover painting by legendary pulp artist Robert McGinnis, creator of the posters for *Breakfast at Tiffany's* and the original Sean Connery James Bond movies.

"[Aleas] gives Chandler a run for his money." — Paramour

Order at www.HardCaseCrime.com or call 1-800-481-9191 (10am to 9pm EST)

...Or Mail in This Handy Order Form:

Dorchester Publishing Co., Inc., P.O. Box 6640, Wayne, PA 19087-8640
5351-9   **$6.99 U.S. ($8.99 Canada)**

Please add $2.50 for shipping and handling for the first book and $0.75 for each book thereafter. NY and PA residents, please add appropriate sales tax. No cash, stamps, or C.O.D.s. All orders shipped within 6 weeks via postal service book rate. Canadian orders require $2.50 extra postage and must be paid in U.S. dollars through a U.S. banking facility. Payment must accompany all orders.

Name _____

Address _____

City _____ State _____ Zip _____

I have enclosed $ _____ in payment for _____ copies of this book.

Two for the Money

By the Bestselling Author of "ROAD TO PERDITION"

MAX ALLAN COLLINS

They don't come any tougher than Nolan — but even a hardened professional thief can't fight off the whole Chicago mafia. So after 16 years on the run, Nolan's ready to let an old friend broker a truce. The terms: Pull off one last heist and hand over the proceeds.

But when things go wrong, Nolan finds himself facing the deadliest double cross of his career. Fortunately, Nolan has a knack for survival — and an unmatched hunger for revenge...

"No one can twist you through a maze with as much intensity and suspense as Max Allan Collins." — Clive Cussler

Order at www.HardCaseCrime.com or call 1-800-481-9191 (10am to 9pm EST)
...Or Mail in This Handy Order Form:

Dorchester Publishing Co., Inc., P.O. Box 6640, Wayne, PA 19087-8640
5353-5 $6.99 U.S. ($8.99 Canada)
Please add $2.50 for shipping and handling for the first book and $0.75 for each book thereafter.
NY and PA residents, please add appropriate sales tax. No cash, stamps, or C.O.D.s. All orders shipped
within 6 weeks via postal service book rate. Canadian orders require $2.50 extra postage and must be
paid in U.S. dollars through a U.S. banking facility. Payment must accompany all orders.

Name _____

Address _____

City _____ State _____ Zip _____

I have enclosed $ _____ in payment for ____ copies of this book.

TheMysteryPlace.com

YOUR WEB SOURCE FOR MYSTERY FICTION

Visit www.TheMysteryPlace.com,
home of the leading short-fiction mystery magazines:

ALFRED MYSTERY MAGAZINE
HITCHCOCK. ®

ELLERY QUEEN ®
MYSTERY MAGAZINE

Log On and You'll Enjoy...

- Full Stories On-Line
- Trivia Contests
- Readers' Forum
- Award Lists
- Book Reviews
- Mystery Puzzles...

And more!

VISIT US AT

www.TheMysteryPlace.com